THE TROPHY WIFE OF A WEALTHY GANGSTA

CANDY MOORE

The Trophy Wife Of A Wealthy Gangsta

Copyright © 2024 by Candy Moore

All rights reserved.

Published in the United States of America.

All rights reserved. No part of this publication may be reproduced, distributed, or transmitted in any form or by any means, including photocopying, recording, or other electronic or mechanical methods, without the prior written permission of the publisher, except in the case of brief quotations embodied in critical reviews and certain other noncommercial uses permitted by copyright law. For permission requests, please contact: www.colehartsignature.com

This is a work of fiction. Names, characters, places, and incidents either are the products of the author's imagination or are used fictitiously. Any resemblance of actual persons, living or dead, businesses, companies, events, or locales is entirely coincidental. The publisher does not have any control and does not assume any responsibility for author or third-party websites or their content.

The unauthorized reproduction or distribution of this copyrighted work is a crime punishable by law. No part of the book may be scanned, uploaded to or downloaded from file sharing sites, or distributed in any other way via the Internet or any other means, electronic, or print, without the publisher's permission. Criminal copyright infringement, including infringement without monetary gain, is investigated by the FBI and is punishable by up to five years in federal prison and a fine of $250,000 (www.fbi.gov/ipr/).

This book is licensed for your personal enjoyment only. Thank you for respecting the author's work.

Published by Cole Hart Signature, LLC.

Mailing List

To stay up to date on new releases, plus get information on contests, sneak peeks, and more,

Go To The Website Below...

www.colehartsignature.com

CHAPTER ONE
CHAOS

My right hand was casually draped over the steering wheel of my Lexus truck. A cigar hung loosely between my fingertips as I bobbed my head in time to the song "Monster."

"*Gossip, gossip. Nigga just stop it. Everybody knows I'm a mothafucking monster.*" I rapped along the words to the song as I drove through the streets of Philly. Whenever I was on my way to a drug deal I always played this song, smoked my cigar, and made sure I had fucked my wife before I left the house.

I played this song because that's what I felt like every time I was about to hand over this work in exchange for a stupid amount of cash...like a mothafucking monster! Even though my name was DeAndre Pereira, in the streets I was known as Chaos. The most infamous drug dealer from the streets of Philadelphia.

I was born and raised in the rough streets of Frankford. At thirty-four years old I'm the oldest of my three siblings. I have two sisters, Danesha who is twenty-three and Daniella who's twenty-six, that I would kill for and they hated it. Simply because when niggas stepped to them and they found out that Chaos was their brother, it was a fucking wrap.

My parents are still married. They did try their best to raise me the right way. I don't have a sad story, like my daddy was a drug dealer who was in and out of prison all my life. Or my momma was strung out on the crack pipe, sucking dick to put food on the table.

Nope, my story was nothing like that. My father was a mechanic who owned his own shop. My mother worked at one of our local banks as a supervisor. My parents are good people, they just had a son that preferred the finer things in life. Like having more than three luxury vehicles parked in front of a four-bedroom, three-bathroom home with an indoor and outdoor pool and a movie and game room. Plus, the husband to the baddest bitch that touched these Philly streets.

Was I supposed to really accomplish that type of lifestyle working a 9 to 5 in some shit job? I don't think so.

My phone started ringing, bringing me out of my thoughts. I sighed softly when I saw it was my wife. She knew I really didn't like to be bothered when I'm about to make a drop. Knowing I was probably going to regret answering, I lowered the music on my radio before I connected the call from my steering wheel.

"Beautyful." I stressed on her name to let her know I didn't particularly like that she was calling me.

"On your way home can you bring me something to eat?" Her smooth, sexy voice filled the inside of my whip, as she was on speaker. I made a face because I just knew I would have regretted this conversation.

"Are you being serious right now?" I asked her, ready to hang the fuck up.

"Why would I call you asking for food and be joking?" she asked in an annoyed voice.

"The fuck, call Uber Eats or some shit. Or better yet, I know you lying in bed, get your ass up and make you something. There's mad food in the kitchen." My voice began to rise because she had a nigga fucked up.

"Firstly, those delivery drivers always forget part of my order or sometimes they even eat my shit, and secondly, if you didn't wear me out like you did before you left, maybe I'd be able to get my sore ass out of this bed and make me a plate," she replied with an attitude. She was spoiled as a mothafucka, but I didn't mind as I was responsible for it.

The last time Beautyful took her ass to the kitchen and made us something, dinosaurs roamed the earth.

What she said made my two niggas who were in the car with me chuckle under their breath. She knew I had her on speaker phone, she just wanted to do the most. I shook my head as I raised the cigar and puffed on it.

"Whether I fucked you good or not, your ass still wasn't about to make shit. I'll call you when I'm on the way back to the crib and you'll tell me what you want," I told her and hung up before she had time to say anything else.

I turned to my nigga in the front seat, Bjorn Harry, who we sometimes called Big B, and he laughed softly. He was used to me and Beautyful and our regular bullshit. Bjorn and I grew up together a couple houses from each other.

Unlike my story, Bjorn's was different. He did not come from a household like mine. In fact, his story was pretty fucked up. His father was murdered when he was just a year old. His momma was a hot crotch that changed niggas like it was going out of style.

Unfortunately, her niggas enjoyed slapping Bjorn around just for the hell of it. Until one day when he was fourteen, he picked up an ice pick and stabbed his mother's latest nigga, Tony, in his hand because he tried to grab his dick. I believed he would have killed that fool hadn't his older sister stopped him.

Bjorn got the nickname Big B because he was taller than a mothafucka. He was the exact replica of the rapper Slim Thug. He was bald headed with a medium brown color and a well maintained, thick beard that he took care of with a shitload of beard products.

"I swear something's wrong with that girl." I chuckled under my breath as I got closer to the spot.

"You know you're about to stop and get her something to eat," Antoine chimed in from the back seat. Lifting my eyes, I looked at him from my rearview mirror as he puffed on a blunt. I ignored what he said, choosing not to discuss what I will and will not do for my wife with just anybody.

Antoine, or Animal as he was nicknamed, was more Bjorn's people than he was mine. He was cool in my book and everything, but I didn't fuck with him as much. Even though he was Bjorn's homeboy, I still preferred to keep him at arm's length.

Antoine's nickname said it all; he was a wild and unhinged mothafucka. He was skinny as fuck with hair that stood on the ends of his head like Kodak Black's. He was dark skinned and rocked top and bottom platinum grills. The only reason I allowed him to be around me on a night like this one was because he had an aim like he trained in the military or CIA or some shit.

Presently, he sat with an AR-15 on his lap, ready for war as always. A Glock 19 was my preference and a Desert Eagle sat between my nigga Bjorn's knees as he texted on his cell.

Reaching over, I raised the volume on the radio and continued bobbing my head to the song. Resetting my mood back to "Monster" as I drove the remainder of the way.

Ok first thing's first, I'll eat your brains
Then I'mma start rocking gold teeth and fangs

'Cause that's what a mothafucking Monster do
Young Money is the rasta from the monster crew.

Five minutes later I yanked the handle of my Lexus door open and hopped out. My camouflage sweatpants hung low on my waist. I adjusted the gun to the back of my boxers before covering it with my matching camouflage jacket. After tucking the bottom of my sweatpants inside my Timberland boots, I closed my door.

Using the palm of my hand, I smoothed the waves of my low fade as I looked over at my boys.

"Grab the duffel bag, Animal," I instructed him so he wouldn't forget the kilos of cocaine hidden in a compartment I made in my vehicle for transporting my illegal shit. Tipping my head back, I blew out the cigar smoke into the cool night's air before dropping it at my feet and then stepping on it.

"Leggo!" I exclaimed to my niggas as I began walking to get this over with. Bjorn nodded at me, following my steps.

Looking at the abandoned warehouse, I held the iced-out pendant that swung from my platinum chain as I began walking. My long legs carried my 6'4" medium-built frame to the entrance of the warehouse with my boys at my side.

Walking inside the dank, dismal, medium-sized empty room, I spotted the niggas I was supposed to do business with. As I got closer to them I scanned the three individuals cautiously.

My eyes settled on the dread-head nigga. He was the person I had to address. Normally, I did transactions with his brother, but he was out of town and he told me that I needed to meet up with his sibling instead.

He got a big, fat fuck no when he suggested that about a week ago because I didn't know his brother. However, Pharaoh, as he's known on the streets, because that was actually his birth name explained that his brother was safe and I had nothing to worry about. I refused profusely because in this drug game, I trusted nobody, and I did mean nobody.

Niggas switched up on you fast as fuck if they believed a bag would come their way if they did. I refused Pharaoh's request of doing business with his brother for three days straight until he called again saying his out of town trip got extended and his niggas' street supply was drying up.

He promised that after this he would never ask me to do business with anybody else again. He also for the hundredth time vouched for his brother, telling me I had nothing to worry about.

Me and Pharaoh had been doing business a little over a year now. I was the only cocaine dealer that got the purest Colombian coke one could lay their finger on. My list of customers was long because of the grade of coke I had. Against my better judgment, I agreed to meet with his brother, so here I was.

Silently, with my hands shoved inside of my camo pants, I studied his sibling, whose name I was told was Moses. Their parents probably were real mothafucking disappointed that they gave their sons biblical names only for them to end up being drug dealers.

Moses looked a little like his brother; he was more on the shorter side of Pharaoh's six feet two inches. Moses was a skinny nigga with eyes that were a little too big for his tiny head. His eyes were on me just as mine were on him.

"Chaos..." he finally addressed me with a raise of his right hand, his index finger pointed at me. A toothpick hung loosely from his lips.

I could give a fuck about an introduction. I turned to one of his boys who held tightly to a duffel bag. I knew these niggas were strapped, I just didn't know what kind of weapons they had on them.

"You got my money?" I asked, looking over at the duffel bag.

"You got my kilos?" he asked, interlocking his fingers, resting them on his upper thighs.

I really didn't do tit for tat, so I signaled for Animal to step forward and display the drugs so this goofy could hand me my fucking money and I could get the fuck on. My eyes fell on the other guy who was just standing there. I tried not to let my face show that I recognized he seemed jittery.

He was moving from one foot to the other and his hands couldn't seem to stay still.

As Animal unzipped the bag and showed the kilos of cocaine wrapped neatly inside clear plastic, I used that opportunity to look at my nigga Big B. His eyes were narrowed at the same nigga I was focused on.

Yeah, something was up. Big B suddenly shifted his eyes to me, and with that look I knew he meant these niggas were on some bullshit.

I spoke with my eyes, letting him know what I had to do. Just as I opened my mouth to announce the deal was fucking off and they all could kick bricks, a hail of gunshots rang out.

"Fuck!" I shouted when I felt a burning sensation in my left leg. The very same jittery nigga had his weapon out, firing like a maniac at us.

"You mothafuckas!" Animal yelled out as he tried to aim his AR at the shooter.

Pow...pow...pow!

Three more shots echoed through the empty warehouse. My weapon was already out as I aimed for Pharaoh's brother who had his gun aimed at me.

Big B began firing, as did I before I turned to make a dash for the way we entered.

"Mothaf—" I cried out when another burning feeling

coursed throughout my body. I tumbled to the ground on my stomach. As I groaned in agony from the immense pain I felt in my leg and my back, I tried futilely to get back up on my feet.

"Arrgggh," I grunted when I realized I had absolutely no feeling in my legs and I couldn't stand. Matter of fact, I had no feeling whatsoever below my waist. Breathing began to feel difficult and painful, as I struggled to fill my lungs with air. I managed to roll onto my back and looked around the warehouse, feeling myself going in and out of consciousness.

A short distance away I could see Animal. His arms and legs spread wide as he laid on his back, his lifeless eyes staring upward. My heart drummed loudly in my ears and then it began to beat in a sluggish rhythm.

I could hear my breathing slow and in the distance, I heard someone call out to me.

"Chaos! Aye, can you hear me?" I felt a hand lift my head as the pain from my gunshot wounds didn't hurt as bad anymore. Instead, my entire body felt numb.

"Chaos!" was the last word I heard before my friend's face looked down at me...and then everything went black.

The voice of someone talking made me stir a little in my sleep. The slow rhythmic sound of a machine beeping had me wondering what was making that noise. I tried to remember what happened. The harder I tried the further away my memory ran.

"Do you think he'll wake up today? It's been three days since he got shot." I knew that voice...it was my wife. Hearing a familiar voice made me want to open my eyes.

"I can't say, Mrs. Pereira. If you'll excuse me, I have other rounds to make," the man said, and then I heard footsteps and a door open. I felt a petite warm hand grab my own.

"Baby, I wish you'd wake up. I miss you so much." I could smell her scent. She bent and kissed my forehead and then placed a light kiss on my lips. Her gentle touch made my eyes flutter and I tried hard to open them.

"Oh my god, DeAndre...baby, can you hear me?" she said and I forced my left eye open. The brightness of the room made me shut that mothafucka just as fast.

"Hey, hey, open your eyes again. Please, baby," she pleaded with me. Just because I loved this woman so much, I tried again.

With a low groan, I cracked both eyes open this time and squinted because my eyeballs hurt like hell.

"Mmm, where am I?" I asked softly, trying to focus on my wife's face. My mouth and throat felt so dry I desperately needed a drink of water.

"You're in the hospital," she replied, stroking my hair tenderly with a sad look on her face. I frowned at her, wondering why I was at the hospital. Looking away from her, my eyes fell on the lower half of my body. My left leg was bandaged and raised off the bed in some kind of contraption. Even though it was wrapped up I could tell it was swollen slightly.

Suddenly my memory came crashing back, and I made a face because it literally hurt my head as I recalled being shot.

"Where's Bjorn?" I asked for my partner in crime.

"He's fine. He wasn't injured in any way." I nodded my head, happy to know my friend was straight. Something didn't feel right though, I couldn't put my finger on it.

"Um, baby, there's something you should know," Beautyful began talking, but then I realized what was off. Why didn't I feel anything in my injured leg where I had gotten shot?

Taking my hands, I began touching the lower half of my body and recoiled in horror when I felt absolutely nothing.

"What the fuck is wrong with me?" I asked frantically, slapping my legs over and over but felt nothing.

"Hey, just relax. It's going to be alright." Beautyful tried to calm me down, but I was losing my shit because I had no feeling in my legs. Everything from the waist down was numb.

"The fuck is this! Why can't I feel anything?" I raised my voice, trying to get up but that also proved to be futile.

"DeAndre, please," Beautyful begged tearfully as she tried to pin me back to the bed.

"Nah, fuck all that. What the fuck is wrong with me?" I flung the covers off my body and my wife hit the button at the side of the bed to signal the nurses that they needed to come to the room.

"Bjornnnn! Where the fuck is my nigga? Bjorn!" I cried out hysterically just as nurses and a doctor came racing into my room.

"Please, baby it's gonna be ok." Beautyful's voice cracked as she cried uncontrollably, stepping back from the bed so that the nurses could get to me.

"Ayo, why can't I feel my legs?" I addressed the nurse who was injecting something into the IV that was in my hand.

"It will be alright, Mr. Pereira," she said softly while another nurse tried to hold my arms down.

"Beautyful, what's wrong with me?" I asked, but all she did was cry even more. Why wasn't anybody answering my question? My eyelids suddenly felt heavy and I could feel them start to close.

My eyes were still on my wife. She wiped her tear-soaked cheeks while she sniffed. I will never forget that look she had on her face. The last thing I heard her say was...

"It's gonna be ok."

CHAPTER TWO
BEAUTYFUL

"Beautyful! I know you hear me calling you! I've been calling you for the past five minutes!"

I sighed softly, closed my eyes, and took a deep calming breath as the piercing sound of my husband's voice echoed through our home. My eyelids flew open before I continued rolling out the pizza dough on the floored board.

"Beautyful!" he barked again, louder, as if I had some sort of hearing problem. I looked down at the rolling pin in my hand and I actually thought about killing that man. Like for a fleeting second, I believed I could murder him by using this rolling pin and clobbering my husband to death.

I loved DeAndre, I really did love him, but for the past three and a half months...I did not like him.

"If you don't want to take care of me you're free to pack your shit and get the fuck out." His voice suddenly sounded behind me, letting me know that he had wheeled himself into the kitchen.

Turning around slowly, I pressed my back into the edge of

the kitchen counter, rolling pin in hand as I looked at the man I loved. I sighed softly.

"Chaos, I'm not about to bring you any alcohol. Which I'm pretty sure that's what you're calling me for," I answered him calmly, not even bothering to acknowledge his stupid, ignorant remark about me leaving our marital home.

"How the fuck do you even know what I want when you didn't even bother to come check on a nigga? I could have been fucking dying and you wouldn't even give a fuck." His handsome face twisted into an angry expression.

The only faces he made recently were angry ones. Always angry, never anything else. The only words he knew for the past few months were bitter and vile ones. I was trying, Lord knows I was trying to be understanding to this man and what he was going through, but he was making it so fucking hard.

"Ok, Chaos." I placed the rolling pin down on the board next to the pizza dough. Just in case I got any ideas to whoop him upside his head with the heavy wooden apparatus. I gave my husband my undivided attention. "What is it you want? How can I help you?"

With an angry gleam in his eyes, he sucked his teeth and ignored my question. Instead, he placed his hands on the wheels of his chair and turned it in motion. Rolling past me, he went to the refrigerator, grabbed the handle, and yanked it open.

I curled my lips in and tried my best not to say anything because I knew in about three seconds he was about to go off again.

"Where the fuck did you put my beer?" he hollered at me before looking over his shoulder. Releasing a frustrated sigh, I went back to the task at hand of rolling out my pizza dough. The fact that I actually picked up cooking spoke volumes. Before DeAndre had been shot, spending time in the kitchen was something I hated. Now, over the last few months, I have actually started enjoying making and creating new meals.

"You don't hear me talking to you?" he asked, wheeling over to where I was after he slammed the door to the refrigerator shut.

"You know you're not supposed to be drinking alcohol with your medication, DeAndre." I used his government name because he needed to know he didn't have much longer with me before I lost my shit.

"Do I look like I give a fuck about my medication? The shit isn't even working because I'm still in this fucking chair. My legs still don't fucking work!" I heard the pain and frustration in his voice. Pausing my rolling, I turned to him.

"Maybe it's because you're not trying. Maybe it's because all you do is complain and feel sorry for yourself. Your paralysis is temporary DeAndre, it's not permanent but you have to put in the work." I can't say how many times I've said these words to him. It just seemed to go in one ear and out the other.

"Feel sorry for myself? I have an idea, how about you come sit in this chair and see how much you fucking like it! I'll holla at my nigga Bjorn to get me some more beer."

Those were his final parting words before he grimaced at me, wheeling himself out of our spacious kitchen. I stood in silence and watched him as he left the room and I shook my head.

Picking up my phone from off the counter, I quickly dialed Bjorn's number and waited for him to answer.

"What's up, Beautyful?" he answered on the third ring.

"He's about to call you. You got two options, either you don't answer or if you do, please tell him no," I instructed DeAndre's childhood friend Bjorn how to deal with the call he was about to get.

"I got you. Did you find another physical therapist yet?" he asked, and I closed my eyes before I answered.

"No, and at this rate, I don't think anybody will be up for the challenge."

Putting the call on speaker, I placed the phone on the counter so I could continue rolling out my dough.

"Hang in there, you'll get somebody soon," Bjorn tried to persuade me. I made a face and rolled my eyes because I knew better.

"Let's hope so. I gotta go," I told him before hanging up the call.

Using my upper body strength, I took all of my frustration out on this pizza dough. My mind was a whirlwind of thoughts because they were heavy on my husband. He had spent almost a month at the hospital but since he found out about his temporary paralysis, he changed...a lot.

Paramyotonia congenita is the type of paralysis my husband was diagnosed with. The doctors said this type of paralysis happens when trauma affects the spinal cord in DeAndre's case his trauma came from a bullet. Throughout the process he would have spastic movement where his muscles would jerk and flinch on their own.

DeAndre was so angry and hurt over what happened that those phantom movements hadn't occurred. It's like his brain didn't allow it to happen because of his negative mannerism.

Even though I didn't want to and as much as I tried to fight my emotions, I felt the corners of my eyes grow misty. Sniffing back the tears, I angrily shoved the rolling pin aside.

Wiping my hand on the apron around my waist, I walked to the fridge and opened it. Snatching my Tumbler bottle with my name written in pink, glitter letters from the second shelf. I hopped on top of the island countertop and took a sip of the wine. Fuck water at this point; the only thing I kept in this plastic bottle was some kind of alcoholic beverage.

DeAndre wasn't supposed to drink alcohol but I sure could. Dealing with that man was slowly turning a bitch into an alcoholic. Reaching for my phone, I decided to take a trip down memory lane as I scanned through my pictures.

A smile tugged at my lips when I found a picture of me and DeAndre nine months ago when we went on vacation in Bora Bora. My cinnamon skin glistened under the sun. My shoulder-length hair clung to my neck as I smiled. The corners of my eyes crinkled as I held up the camera while my husband playfully bit into my cheek just before I took the picture, catching me off guard. The expression on both our faces showed just how much we loved each other.

I admired my body in the two-piece bikini. I was more on the slim side but my body was curvy and I had a nice ass. I kept in shape with Yoga and pole dancing classes. However, since DeAndre had been shot, I lost a bit of weight and have been desperately trying to gain it back.

I will never forget that night for as long as I live. When Bjorn called me just as I started to drift off to sleep, his voice hysterical saying the deal went left and DeAndre had been shot along with Bjorn's friend Animal who didn't make it.

I remember getting dressed and driving to the hospital as though I was in some sort of trance. Bjorn tried his best to comfort me once he got done telling me that DeAndre had been paralyzed.

The bullet damaged a nerve in his spinal cord and it would take intense physical therapy to get his legs working again. All of that was fine except DeAndre did not take the news of losing his ability to walk temporarily well.

As the days passed, he grew angry and bitter. Barking at

the doctors, nurses, and not to mention I got the shitty end of it the most. He was angry with the world and felt sorry for himself. Revenge was on his mind for the man named Pharaoh who organized the deal. His men had been killed that night also, one being his brother Moses.

I didn't know much about what happened because DeAndre never shared his illegal business transactions with me. All I knew was shit went left, Pharaoh's men pulled on DeAndre and his crew, and in the end only Bjorn and my husband left that warehouse alive.

I kept scrolling through the pictures, going all the way back to our first date when he took me to a Waffle House after he learned I'd never been there. I smiled at the memory of the shocked look on his face when I told him that.

DeAndre and I met six years ago when I was just twenty-five years old. My father gave me his car to drive that particular day. My sister Lovely and I went to kick it at the mall. When we returned to the parking lot some fucking loser had hit the side of our father's parked car.

I remember being so hysterical, I damn near had a panic attack as I told my sister our father would kill me. I was the youngest between Lovely and I, so he trusted me that one time to drive and that shit happened.

Lovely told me not to panic and made a few calls. She got the address of a mechanic shop not far from the mall where we were and hastily we made our way over there.

The mechanic who owned the shop was Joseph Pereira. I remember he was so nice to me and sympathetic after I told him my father would skin me alive even though it wasn't my fault. He told me he would have it fixed and we didn't even need to leave it and come back, he would fix it on the spot. My sister and I sat out front of his shop and waited.

As we sat talking, a black new series BMW pulled up. Me

and my sister stopped talking because the rap music from inside the car was so loud. The passenger door opened first and out stepped this tall mothafucka, he was just tall for no goddamn reason. His beard was short, well maintained, and looked like he took a lot of pride in it. He rocked a really low haircut, almost bald. Tattoos littered both of his arms and his jeans hung off his waist. I could tell he probably sold drugs. He gave off that Philly dopeboy vibe.

He eyed my sister briefly before he began to walk inside of the mechanic shop. Then the driver's door opened and out stepped the most handsome man I swore I'd ever seen in my life.

Soon as he stepped out of his car he took a cigarette from behind his ear and lit it. Using the palm of his right hand he smoothed out the waves of his low-fade haircut. I recall tucking my lower lip between my teeth as I lusted at this perfect stranger.

Tipping his head back, he blew out his cigarette smoke in the air before his eyes fell on me. His face was expressionless as he looked me over in my pair of jean shorts and a simple Baby Phat t-shirt. On my feet were a pair of plain black sandals.

I didn't come from money. My father worked as a correctional officer and my mother passed away when I was twenty from kidney failure. I recently started working as a secretary at a doctor's office.

I really wanted to look away as he walked past me but I just couldn't. His black jeans fell neatly on his medium-sized lower half and his Polo t-shirt showed off his toned, upper body. He had a colorful tattoo sleeve on his right hand, he even had tattoos wrapped around his neck. Gleaming in the sun was an iced-out chain with an equally iced-out pendant with the name Chaos.

His belt buckle also had the same name his pendant carried

in cursive writing. I was pretty sure those were real diamonds in his belt buckle. As he passed me and my sister, I got a whiff of his masculine cologne and I wanted to melt into the ground.

He followed the taller guy inside of the mechanic shop and a couple minutes after, they both emerged again. Just as suddenly as they appeared they both hopped back into the car they came in and drove off.

That was it, they just disappeared again, but the way he and his companion vanished made me sad for some reason. His presence was so strong that I thought about him for days to come after. I wished I would accidentally bump into him again, but it never happened.

Just when I finally began to forget about him, I was seated behind the desk of the office where I worked and in walked a middle-aged woman with kind eyes.

She gave me her name and sat waiting for her appointment time so she could go in to see the doctor. Ten minutes later I escorted her into the room and took my seat again behind the desk. Leisurely I played solitaire on the desktop computer because it was a slow day.

I swear I didn't hear the door open, so the sound of someone speaking almost made me catch a heart attack.

"Is my moms back there?" I gasped softly at the deep, somewhat raspy, sexy voice. When I looked up from my computer screen I froze for a few seconds. It was him.

Our eyes connected and I could see him mentally trying to place my face. I stayed staring at him like I was a fucking mute for a few seconds before I finally found my voice.

"Um, d-do you mean Mrs. Pereira?" I asked him.

"Yeah, she's back there?" His voice was both sexy and gruff at the same time.

"Yes, she should be out within the next few minutes." I tried to keep my voice steady and not sound as though I was fidgeting from being so nervous. I got a whiff of his cologne and was reminded of the first time I saw him. His fragrance was so masculine and sensual, it did something to my insides just like on the first day I smelled him.

Today he was dressed in a khaki jacket that was unbuttoned with a white t-shirt underneath, and his Chaos iced-out pendant swung across the white background of his clothing. The matching khaki pants hung low on his hip, showing off his medium-built physique.

"Aite bet," he answered and took a seat on one of the chairs in the waiting area. Picking up a year-old magazine on the small circular table, he rested his elbows on his knees with the magazine low between his legs as he flipped through the pages. I knew he wasn't reading shit but he sure looked cute doing it.

God alone knows how I tried to keep my eyes off that man, but every chance I got my vision drifted over at him. By my third glance he was looking back at me.

Shit, I cursed in my head, quickly averting my eyes back to the game that I was currently losing.

"Where do I know you from? Why yo' face seem so familiar?" His deep, sexy voice made the hairs on my arms stand up. Shyly, I looked up at him and he licked his lips with the tip of his tongue waiting for my answer.

"Um, I th-think it's from the mechanic shop almost two weeks ago. I was there with my sister and you came with another guy. Really tall..." I put my hand in the air to emphasize the word tall.

He narrowed his eyes briefly and then he smiled with recognition as his memory of that day came back.

"Oh yeah," was his only reply before he plucked a toothpick from behind his ear and placed it into his mouth. Tossing the magazine back on the table, he hopped to his feet and walked back toward my desk.

My eyes grew wide as he sauntered in my direction. I wiggled nervously on my chair and I swore I forgot how to breathe. Matter of fact I felt as though I would pass out, then won't that be fucking embarrassing. Imagine me falling off this chair sprawled out unconscious because this nigga was too fine for his own good.

"What's your name?" he asked, playing with his hands as he studied me.

"I'm Beautyful Daye," I replied softly. I never really liked my name. I always thought it was stupid. My sister Lovely was older than me by three years. Lovely Daye was the name given to her by my father, Kenneth Daye. The reason for her name was because the song "Lovely Day" by Bill Withers was playing at a wedding while my mother and father danced.

My mother's water broke, signaling she was in labor about to bring their first child into the world. My father thought that the name Lovely was suited for my sister because of the song that played ushering her on earth. Seeing that my father's last name was Daye, he believed the name was absolutely perfect for her. When my parents had me they decided to stick with the theme, unfortunately, and named me Beautyful Daye. The stupid jokes when I attended high school were endless.

"The name suits you." He smiled at me, showing an even set of lily-white teeth. I bent my head as I blushed like crazy. The door to the doctor's office suddenly opened and out stepped Mrs. Pereira, his mother.

"Hey, Mama. What the doctor say? You pregnant or what?" he cracked, which his mother didn't find amusing. Sucking her teeth, she flashed me a warm smile as she began walking.

"Pay the lady and stop being an ass, DeAndre."

I stifled a laugh. I liked his mother. Not to mention thanks to her, I had a name to the face, DeAndre. This perfect man's name was DeAndre. It made me wonder how he got the nickname Chaos that he wore so proudly around his neck and his waist.

Yanking out a shitload of money from his pocket, he dropped a crisp hundred-dollar bill on the table.

"See ya later, Beautyful," he said, with a wink of his right eye as he walked away. I was so lost in his handsome face, his intoxicating cologne, and his swag, I forgot his mother's visit was only $80.

"Hey, your change!" I shouted at him as I got up from the chair, leaning against the desk and waving the $20 bill at him. DeAndre lifted his right arm, as if to say he didn't want it as he kept it pushing out the door.

Curling my lips in, I watched and blushed as he walked next to his mother, and for the second time...he walked out of my life. At least I had a name this time.

The ringing of the phone in my hand brought me back to the present. Sighing loudly, I smiled when my sister's name popped up on the screen that sat on the countertop.

Swiping at the screen enthusiastically up the phone, I answered her call.

"Hey, Lovely."

"I just know DeAndre's ass is wrecking your damn nerves. Meet me and Toni at our regular spot in the next hour." She didn't even give me the chance to say shit else before she hung up the phone.

Shit, she didn't have to tell a bitch twice. Throwing the remainder of alcohol down the back of my throat, I hopped off the counter.

Grabbing the pizza dough and the floured board, I walked over to the refrigerator and shoved them both inside. Once I closed the fridge door shut I stood and looked in the direction of where DeAndre wheeled himself off and took a deep breath.

A shit storm was about to break out when I told him I was about to go meet up with my sister and my friend.

"Fuck it," I said to nobody as I began walking out of the kitchen. "Bring on the mothafucking fireworks."

CHAPTER THREE
CHAOS

I was agitated as fuck as I sat in this fucking stupid fucking wheelchair while attempting to roll a blunt on my lap. The sight of my legs made me angry to the point where I wanted to grab a chainsaw and cut these shits off myself.

Every day instead of focusing on making my legs work again, I would be focused on revenge. The only thing that drove me, the only thing that made me wake up each morning, was knowing one day I would get the opportunity to pump and empty my clip in Pharaoh's mothafucking head.

I rubbed my chin, the hair that covered my face was out of control as well as the hair on top my head. I needed a haircut and mark-up in the worst way, but I could give a fuck about my appearance. With my grinder in hand I went to work as I looked up, hearing the sound of footsteps.

My wife walked into the living room that I sat in and without giving me so much as a second glance, marched up the stairs. I knew she would have called Bjorn and warned him about wanting him to bring me beer. Which was why I didn't even bother to make the call. I shook my head as I eyed her petite but curvy body. She could be mad all she wants, she wasn't the one seated in a chair with noodles for legs.

Thinking about my legs always brought me back to the night all of this happened. I knew Pharaoh set me up. He was hoping by having his brother eliminate me that he would be able to finally get a way around to my connect. The connect that had the best cocaine money could buy. I was the only one that had cocaine straight from Colombia and Pharaoh wanted my connect so fucking bad the nigga got greedy and vengeful.

So what does he do? He tried to get his brother, Moses, to kill me and it backfired because his brother was a whole mothafucking goofy. Instead, Moses ended up dead lying six feet under somewhere and so did Bjorn's friend, Animal. Not to mention I got a bullet in my leg and back that fucked up my spinal cord.

As if being temporarily paralyzed wasn't enough, me and Bjorn have been trying to locate Pharaoh for the last three months and that nigga done turned into a ghost. He knew he was a dead man walking. Once I found him, it would be a wrap. Bjorn wanted Pharaoh just as bad for him whacking Animal.

Bjorn and I had eyes just about everywhere. We had niggas on high alert with strict instructions to let us know that if Pharaoh was spotted anywhere, at any time, they had to get word back to us. So far all we heard was that he went to fucking Greece or Italy or some shit, and that he didn't plan on ever returning to the US.

I never believed that bullshit out of the country rumor. Pharaoh was a calculated sort of nigga. We killed his brother, and he would want revenge for that shit. My guard had to be up at all times, because he could pounce at any second. Na, I didn't believe that nigga was in another country at all. He was right here planning and scheming on how he would get back at me and Bjorn for killing his blood.

I prayed to God that when he did, I would be healed and would have regained mobility in my legs again. Yanking the lighter from out my sweatpants pocket, I sparked up my joint and inhaled deeply as I looked at the staircase.

The smoke cloud from my blunt blurred my vision a little as I stared at the mechanism Beautyful had some contractors come and attach to the side of the staircase.

I grew angry again at what I called the wheelchair slide, the proper name being a stairlift. I had to sit on the chair at the side, hold the remote, and then that mothafucka would glide me along to the top of the stairs. The shit was slow as fuck, and then my wife was supposed to bring my wheelchair up for me.

Beautyful had those contractors come construct this shit without my knowledge and consent. I was out with Bjorn on that particular day. He took me to my parents' house because they wanted me to come see them. When I got home, Beautyful was standing next to the stairs with a big stupid smile on her face. I was confused as a mothafucka when she shouted *surprise* while pointing at the staircase.

"The fuck is that?" I asked her, my face already showing signs that I was annoyed.

"It's a mechanical stair climber or a stairlift. It's to help you up and down the stairs so you won't need to sleep down here in the guest bedroom again," she explained, and I could tell she was taken aback by the way I was looking at her.

"Don't you like it?"

"The fuck! What, you think I plan on being in this chair for the rest of my fucking life? Why in the fuck would you go and put some shit like this to the staircase without asking for my permission, no doubt!" I yelled at her as she cowered back from my insults.

"Aye, relax Chaos." Bjorn came from behind the chair so he could stand in front of me. He looked down at me with a pissed off look.

"All y'all were in on this fuck shit. That's why my parents had me visit them so I would be out of the house all day. While my wife prepared for me to remain a cripple for the rest of my life!"

I pulled the hair on my jaw as the memory replayed in my head, knowing that I overreacted to a gesture that was supposed to have been thoughtful. Absentmindedly, I bobbed my head to the music that played from the Echo Dot that sat on top of the glass center table.

I know since the accident I have been anything but the loving husband to my wife. The anger I felt about my situation always reared its ugly head when Beautyful tried to come to my assistance in any way. I knew she didn't deserve all the arguments I purposely picked, the way I would complain about absolutely nothing. She didn't even deserve my reaction to the stairlift. She had them attach that to the stairs to make shit easier for me. Meanwhile, my reaction was nothing short of a slap to her face.

On top of everything, I barely wanted to take care of my appearance and I was drinking like a nigga whose wife left him with four kids to go live with her new nigga. I was surprised I hadn't fucking died by the way I was mixing my meds with alcohol. I done lost count of the many times Beautyful had to attend to my drunk ass passed out in this chair. I almost fucked around and killed myself one time mixing my antibiotics with two glasses of Hennessey.

Mopping up vomit, having to change my disgusting clothing that I threw up on while she struggled to get me out of the chair and under the shower. She did all of that and to be honest, I never really heard her complain or raise her voice at me...not once. The only thing she would say was that I had to do better and stop feeling sorry for myself.

I mean, I wasn't even sleeping in our bedroom because I refused to allow her to assist me up and down those stairs. Even though she said she was able and didn't mind, to me that shit was fucking embarrassing. My wife trying to have me hold on to her shoulders as she tried to drag my ass up the stairs was not on my to-do list. Hence the reason she had the stairlift installed.

Even then I still refused to use it because I was too much of a proud man. The only way I would be going up those stairs was with my own two feet going one in front of the other.

So instead, I slept downstairs in the guest bedroom, completely neglecting our marital bed. I would fall asleep alone and would always awaken to Beautyful curled up against me in the middle of the night. I would watch her sleep as she snored softly, contented to be next to her husband. She often told me she slept better with me by her side.

Sometimes I would admire her wearing one of my t shirts that fit her tiny body like a parachute. I wanted her so badly that every bone in my body ached. Sex was something we had only a handful times since the shooting. As much as I yearned for my wife having her climb on top of me every time we had to fuck, shit made me feel like less of a man.

Sighing softly, I felt my frustration building again because I did love my wife and I knew she was trying...but I was just so fucking angry. Suddenly, a familiar song started playing from the Echo speakers. I used my index and thumb to tug at my lower lip as I listened to the words at the beginning of the song.

Let me know, let me know
When I feel, what I feel
Sometimes it's hard to tell you so

You may not be in the mood to learn what you think you know.

Aaliyah's angelic voice filled up the room as she sang "Let Me Know."

With the blunt to my lips, I inhaled deeply before dipping my head back and blowing the white cloud over my head into the air. The memory that this song brought back did something I hadn't done in a while. It made me smile.

This was the song that Beautyful and I danced to on our wedding day, it was our song. The reason for us choosing this particular song to dance to was actually an interesting story.

The first time I laid eyes on my wife was that day at my dad's mechanic shop. She caught my attention for sure, but that day I was busy and had a lot of shit to do. So, hollering at her was absolutely out of the question. A nigga had money to make, money was my driving force in those days. Money and power was all a nigga wanted.

Then we saw each other again when I went to pick my mother up from her doctor's appointment. I recognized her immediately even though I didn't act like it. Against my better judgment, I walked out of the office that day without getting her number. I just had her name...Beautyful. Her name suited her because she was prettier than a mothafucka.

"Shawty gonna be there tonight?" Bjorn asked as he drove us to some party that I didn't even wanna go to in the first place. This nigga was always dragging me to some bullshit when all I really wanted to do was keep a low profile and think of new ways to get my money up.

Currently, I was trying to get a connect that had the best and purest cocaine. The connect's name was Julio and he was from Colombia. The cocaine he fucked with was crazy and off the charts. I just knew if it hit the streets, niggas would go stupid to get their hands on it. In my heart I believed if I could get that Colombian to add me as one of his customers, I was about to shut Philly all the way down. Which was exactly what I wanted to be, the biggest drug dealer Philly ever saw. That kind of power was the shit I dreamed of every night.

"Which shawty we talking about here?" I asked uninterested, smoothing the waves in my hair with the palm of my hand.

"Rochelle, I heard you talking to her on the phone earlier," Bjorn explained as he turned down the street where the house party was being held.

"Fuck, I hope she won't be there. She dick rides hard as hell. She been tryna get me to fuck her without a rubber on. She must think I'm a toddler to this game and don't know when a trick tryna trap a nigga with a baby." Rochelle was the usual type that was attracted to bad boys or dope boys. If you were a bad boy, which she preferred, and your pockets were fat, the more she swore she loved a nigga and you'd get to drop them drawers for sure.

I stifled a yawn as Bjorn slowed his car down in front of the two-story house. Loud rap music blasted from inside as a shitload of people were scattered outside the front of the yard. Popping the collar of my black Lacoste shirt, I opened my door once Bjorn parked alongside the curb.

Doing a quick check of my attire, I adjusted my all-black Levi's to the top of my Timberland boots. The night lights outside bounced off my iced-out Chaos pendant that hung around my neck. The tattoo sleeve on my right hand glistened under the moonlit night. Shoving my hands inside of my pockets, I stood and waited for Bjorn who was talking to some Haitian niggas who just pulled up like us.

I looked at the house and immediately took in the partygoers to see if I made out any familiar faces. I was selling drugs for about five years now and even though money wise I wasn't where I wished I'd be, I wasn't doing too bad. Therefore, I had started making a name for myself and my face was somewhat starting to be one that got recognized. Sometimes that could either be a good or a bad thing.

"Leggo," Bjorn said, which was a word we used whenever we were ready to walk off somewhere. He appeared next to me as he tapped me on my shoulder. We both walked side by side into the yard and I could feel a few females' eyes on us as we walked toward the front door.

This house belonged to one of Bjorn's cousins, Clyde. He did time for armed robbery and came out of prison two years ago. He managed to turn his life around and started his own exotic ice-cream business. Next thing I knew this nigga blew up larger than life. He had actors and actresses, singers and rappers demanding he come to their parties or fancy galas and shit to cater their event with his off the chain ice-cream flavors. Pretty sure he was a millionaire by now.

His house had at least five bedrooms and four bathrooms with a small pool at the back. Even though he was now a rich mothafucka, he never forgot where he came from. This party was filled with dopeboys, drug dealers, hood niggas, and bitches hoping to bag them a wealthy thug.

DMX's song "Party Up" was blasting loud as fuck as we stepped inside the dimly lit room. The weed smoke slapped me in the face like a hooker that came up short with her pimp's money once we made our way into the living room.

Resting my palm against my Chaos pendant to stop it from swinging, I dapped up a couple of dope boys I knew from around the way. The inside of Clyde's house was packed pretty tight. My gun was tucked in my waist because you never knew when shit might pop off.

Bjorn soon found his cousin Clyde and his wife Suzette, a big tittie red bone that had been his day one from ever since. Clyde and I gave one another a brotherly hug before I turned and smiled at his wife in greeting. Truth be told, I had a lot of respect for this nigga. He beat the odds and made something of himself when he got out of prison, and I could respect that.

Bjorn told me the ice-cream business idea came from his shawty, Suzette. She toyed around with a bunch of flavors and would use her friends and family members as guinea pigs for feedback on the taste.

Clyde gave a bottle of Hennessy each to both me and Bjorn before him and his wife turned to mingle with their guests.

"Aye, nigga," he stopped walking to turn and address me. "I know your name is Chaos and all, but let your nickname be *chill* tonight. I don't want to be breaking up any brawls, ya feel me," Clyde joked, before he resumed his steps and walked away with his wife.

Bjorn and I kicked it quietly by ourselves for most of the night, always making sure to stay alert as we drank our alcohol and entertained a few females who decided to come holla at us.

Rarely did I ever approach females. The way this shit worked for me, bitches usually approached me, which made my job ten times easier. I was lazy as fuck when it came to hollering at females. That was only because women stayed on my dick and made me put in little effort to get the pussy. It was always handed to me. Not that I was bragging or anything, but it is what it is.

Roughly an hour or two had passed and I was definitely over this. A nigga was ready to call it a mothafucking night. Not to mention I had managed to drink the entire bottle of Hennessy; Clyde gave me and I was buzzed as hell.

Thank goodness Bjorn was the one driving and not me. I rubbed my eyes and decided as soon as Bjorn got back from the bathroom break he took, I was about to tell him I was ready to dip.

The DJ suddenly changed the music from hip-hop to R&B. I sucked my teeth wondering who asked him for this shit. Scanning the crowd as people began to couple off so they could slow dance, I spotted Rochelle and cursed my bad luck. I began to make my way through a few slow dancing couples because the last thing I needed was for shawty to spot me. As I approached a few people I had to stop and do a double take because I swore, I saw a familiar face.

My eyes darted back and zoomed in on a female as she stood in the corner. She looked a little out of place to me, almost as though she was wondering what she was doing here.

I recognized her as the chick from the doctor's office. I stood and stared at her from a safe distance as she sang along to the lyrics of TLC's song "Waterfalls." Out of all the females that were at the party at this very moment, Beautyful was the only one that stood out to me.

She wore her hair in a high ponytail, and the denim dress she wore was way too short, had no sleeves, and hugged her body tight as hell. Showing off her slim curvaceous body. I remained in a trance when the girl next to her spoke in her ear. I could tell the girl was her sister because they looked alike. She was with her that day when I saw her for the first time at my father's mechanic shop.

Whatever her sister said made her shake her head repeatedly, but her sister waved her off. Next thing I knew, some buster looking nigga was all up in her face.

Let me know, let me know
When I feel, what I feel
Sometimes it's hard to tell you so
You may not be in the mood to learn what you think you know.

A real soulful song started up, I believed it was Aaliyah singing, and I could tell the nigga was asking her to dance.

The possessiveness I felt for this female was fucking

crazy, because I did not want her to dance with this fool. Before I knew what I was doing, my feet had a mind of their own.

Maybe the alcohol had something to do with it because stepping to females just wasn't something I did much, but before I could give more thought to it, I was right there...right next to her.

The goofy that was in her ear saw when she suddenly froze and her eyes were locked in a trance because somebody else had caught her attention.

Looking over his shoulder, his eyes scanned me with curiosity. What was understood didn't need to be said. He got the fucking picture when he saw the look on my face and kept it pushing. This was our third time meeting. It was me and Beautyful once again in each other's presence. We just stood and kind of gawked awkwardly at each other.

"I think I owe you $20," she said with a smile just like her name.

Stepping closer to her so I could close the gap between us, I pressed my lips against her ear.

"If I can have this dance, we'll call it even," I asked and then pulled back so I could look into her pretty brown eyes waiting for an answer.

"You never even told me your name," she said with one of her eyebrows cocked in the air. I smiled at her genuinely because she was so mothafucking pretty. Plus, I was certain she heard when my mother addressed me that day at the office. She was probably just fucking with me, but I played along.

"I'm DeAndre, but as you can tell, I go by the nickname Chaos," I told her, holding my pendant up to her face.

"Um, excuse you, all up in my sister's face. Who are you?" I turned to the voice on my right and her sister was mean mugging me as she looked me up and down, acting like she could drop me on my back.

"DeAndre, this is my sister, Lovely. Please don't pay her any mind," Beautyful introduced us. Plastering my winning smile on my lips, I held my hand out to her in greeting. Narrowing her eyes at me in a somewhat comical way, she shook my hand. They had the two most unique names I've heard in a minute. Beautyful and Lovely Daye, I just knew it had a story behind those names and I couldn't wait to hear it.

"I got my eyes on you," she warned me using her index and middle fingers she pointed at her eyes then to mine. Just as a nigga came up and asked her to dance. She quickly forgot about me and wrapped her arms around homeboy's neck.

Turning my attention back to Beautyful, I licked my lips as I waited for her to answer my question.

"Well?"

"Well what?" she asked playfully.

"Can I have this dance?" I asked for a second time against her ear.

"Alright, I guess so. Since I don't have your $20 on me after all."

I smiled at what she said because she played too much. Leaning in closer, I took her hands and placed them on my shoulders before wrapping my hands around her petite waist, bringing her warm body into mine.

I couldn't stop staring at her, she had a nigga hypnotized. I felt as though if she asked me for my debit card number, social security number, and the keys to my house at this very moment, I would have given it to her without a second thought.

"What you even doing here?" I asked her.

"My sister got invited and she asked me and our friend Toni to come with her. This isn't really my kind of thing so much," she replied with a shrug of her shoulders. The tips of her fingers unintentionally brushed the nape of my neck lightly and my insides erupted.

Fuck, what was this girl doing to me?

"What's your kind of thing then? If you're not much of a house party kind of girl," I asked her, wanting to know every detail I could about her.

"Umm, I like nice quiet things. You know, like a movie, a nice restaurant maybe." I nodded my head, taking a mental note.

"Word, I hear you. I wasn't going to come here tonight but now I'm glad that I did," I told her, and she blushed before tucking her bottom lip between her teeth.

Everything she did was both erotic and timid at the same time, which was sexy as fuck to me.

"Me and you are about to be married one day," I told her, backing her into the wall behind us.

"What?" she laughed softly as she looked up at me as though I was a complete mad man.

There was not the slightest smile, smirk, or grin on my face. I was dead ass, so I repeated my words again.

"Yeah, me and you are about to be married one day. I'm about to be your husband and you're about to be my wife. I'll make you my trophy wife too. I'll give you the mothafucking world so you wouldn't have to work a day in your life if you wanted to." It may have sounded funny to her but when I set my mind to something, you best believe a nigga will achieve it.

"Oh yeah? I'm not so sure I want to be a trophy wife. I like earning my own money, sir," she said to me as I pressed the lower half of my body into hers. I wanted her to feel how much of an effect she was having on me. She needed to feel how hard she was making me without coming off as a creep.

"That's cool if you want to work, but I would prefer to spoil the shit outta you," I replied with a slight nod of my head.

But at your best, you are love,
Yes, you're a positive motivating force within my life
Should you ever feel the need to wonder why
Let me know, let me know.

As Aaliyah sang her song, everyone else in the room disappeared. It was just Beautyful and I as we swayed to the music. The mixture of the Henny, her perfume, and the seductive song had a nigga feeling some sort of way.

Dipping my head, I slowly inched my face closer to hers and I breathed a sigh of relief when she allowed my lips to gently brush across her full, pouty mouth. Wrapping her arms tightly around my neck, she breathed in before releasing a low moan.

Pressing her back into the wall, my actions became even more demanding and bold. As my tongue took dominance over her mouth, twisting and twirling around her own, my right hand inched up her inner thigh and found the outside of her cotton panties.

I pulled my mouth away from hers because I wanted to look in her eyes as I let my fingers invade her warm, sweet wetness.

Nobody paid us any mind. Everyone was lost in their own shameless behavior, similar to the one that I was presently partaking in.

Beautyful's lips parted slowly as I watched her intently while I played with her wet pussy from behind her thin cotton underwear.

Licking my lips, I slowly shifted the material to the left and found her clit.

"Mmmm," she moaned just loud enough for me to hear.

Yeah, I am definitely going to make shawty mine, I thought as she moved her hips against my fingers. My free hand was above her head, pressed against the wall, trapping her in while I used my index and middle finger to dip in and out of her tightness with the rhythm of the song being played.

"You really are beautiful, you know that?" I spoke to her as I continued to show her with my fingers why she was about to be mine but she just didn't know it yet.

As she closed her eyes, her mouth formed a silent O when my middle finger circled her clit with a quickness.

"You got the wettest pussy a nigga ever felt. I bet this shit tastes off the mothafucking chain. I wanna stick my tongue in it, play with it, suck on it until it pulses so hard it hurts. I want you to buss in my mouth," I began spitting my shit because I was about to use both my words and my hand to make her cream on my fingers. I was about to make her cum so fucking hard, she would feel like she was about to pass the fuck out.

"You think you'll like it if I eat this pussy?" I whispered, making sure to keep focus on how much she was enjoying what I was doing to her.

"Y-yessss," she breathed out, nodding her head up and down like a bobble head doll.

"Na, you'll fucking *love* it when I eat this pussy. When I suck on this mothafucking clit. Pull on it a little with my lips before I circle it over and over with the tip of my tongue." My words did their magic while my fingers moved like lightning between her legs.

Beautyful began panting and I felt her nub grow hard under my fingertips. Snatching my shoulders, her mouth opened, her head tilted backward, and I knew she was about to scream. Quickly, I covered her mouth with my own and kissed her deeply as her body trembled profusely from her orgasm.

I gave her the time she needed to float down from her high.

I never let her go as she slowly regained her composure and opened her eyes.

"Oh my god. What the fuck is wrong with me?" she asked, with a look on her face that said she was embarrassed for allowing me to do what I just did. My dick was rock hard in my jeans, but it was cool for now. I'd deal with getting this nut out when I convinced her to leave this party with me.

I took a small step back as she adjusted her clothing, yanking her dress down. Her wetness began to dry from off the tips of my fingers. I wanted to suck on my fingers so bad. Instead, I just flicked the tip of my tongue quickly on my index finger for a little taste of her.

"Nothing's wrong with you. We did what two consenting adults do," I told her with a sly smile.

"I barely even know you. Jesus, I don't even know if you have a girlfriend or not." Beautyful covered her face as though she was mortified. I found her reaction cute and I smiled.

Just as I was about to take my phone out so I could get her number, I felt someone suddenly yanking me by my shoulder. I spun around with my right hand already balled into a fist. I was ready to knock whoever was behind me the fuck out.

I turned to face Bjorn's cousin, Clyde, who had a frantic expression on his face.

"Ayo, go get yo' nigga. He's about to start a fight out in the mothafucking front yard," Clyde said, not even giving me a chance to say anything. He kept pulling on my elbow. Releasing an irritated sound from the back of my throat, I wondered how in the fuck Bjorn was about to fight when he went to use the bathroom. Looking back at Beautyful, I reached for her upper arms and gave them a light squeeze.

"I'll be right back. They don't call me Chaos for nothing," I boasted before reaching for the gun tucked in my waist. "Don't leave, alright. I need to get your number," was the last thing I told her before I ran off with Clyde to find my boy.

That night Bjorn and I got into it with some drunk niggas. I fought like I was trained by Muhammad Ali. Knocking niggas out left and right. When I got tired of using my fists, I shot a couple shots in the air. That was a bad fucking idea because it caused pure mayhem, making the crowd inside and outside to scatter.

I did go back to look for her but she was no longer there. I searched that party high and low, from top to bottom. However, I couldn't find Beautyful and for the third time...we lost touch. I never got her number and then two days later, I got the call that would change my life.

The connect I wanted, Julio, that I needed to put me on game invited me to Colombia. I jumped at the opportunity and Bjorn and I hopped on a plane and were gone for the next three months. The next time I saw Beautyful wouldn't be for another year, and by that time she was in an entire relationship with some lame ass nigga.

The sound of footsteps descending the stairs brought me back to the present. I narrowed my eyes in pure disbelief when they settled on my wife who was dressed as though she was about to go some damn where.

I flicked the tip of my nose with my middle finger in annoyance as she walked my way.

"I'll be back in maybe an hour and a half at the latest. Do you need me to do anything for you before I leave?" she asked me, with cautious steps toward my chair.

An amused look settled on my face as I looked up at her.

"Where the fuck you going dressed like a hooker?" I spat, knowing damn well I was talking shit. She wore a pair of fitted jeans, black thigh-high boots, and a simple fitted black shirt.

She looked very nice and respectful...nothing like a hooker as I insinuated.

"What?" Beautyful gasped, looking down at what she was wearing before looking back at me. "I do not look like that Chaos, you so full of shit," she replied, cutting her eyes at me in disgust. Shocked that I would take it that far.

"I'm still waiting to hear where the fuck you think you're going. You just about to leave me here on my own? You don't even care if I have an accident or not, if I need your help or not." One thing I had mastered over the last three-plus months was picking a fight with my wife and making her feel bad in the process like she had done me wrong. When in reality she hadn't done a thing to me.

Another thing she always offered to do was take me out so I could get out of the house. She brought that shit up a good four times before I eventually cussed her out so bad, she never brought it up again. Why would I want to leave the house in a fucking wheelchair? It was a hard no for me. So instead, I stayed holed up in the house like a fucking hermit crab.

"I'm going out with Lovely and Toni. Please, don't try the guilt trip thing on me. I've been trying to get you help and you keep chasing everyone off, Chaos. I just need an hour to myself and I promise I'll be right back. I called Bjorn to come chill with you and he said he'll be right over, he's less than fifteen minutes away."

I scowled at her and felt nothing but betrayal. She got to have a life, she got to leave when she wanted and do what she pleased. Meanwhile, I was stuck in this fucking chair. Life sure was kicking me in the ass and I was sick of it.

"If you walk out that door, especially dressed as though you about to look for another nigga, don't bother coming back home. Stay your ass with your sister and Toni's hoe ass!" I barked at her, trying to intimidate her with my aggressiveness. It didn't work though.

Exhaling loudly, Beautyful pinched the bridge of her nose before she focused on me. "I'm not doing this with you today. Bjorn will be here soon and I'll be back in an hour or less. Maybe you should think about changing your God-awful ways while I'm gone. I'll see you later," she said before bending and placing an unwanted kiss in the middle of my forehead.

I tried to pull back from her lips but she just grabbed my face and kissed me anyway. I grinded my jaw in rage as I heard the front door open and close behind her.

I aggressively pulled on my blunt until I felt the sides of my cheeks cave in. Taking my cell phone out of my pants pocket, I dialed Bjorn's number.

"Ayo, whadup? I'm on my way to you right now, my boy," he answered after the first ring.

Narrowing my eyes while I listened to him speak, I blew out a thick puff of marijuana smoke into the air.

"Yeah, hurry up. I need you do a nigga a favor right quick," I said before I hung up my phone. My wife thought she was about to play in my face with another nigga, she had another think coming.

I don't give a fuck if I was being paranoid or not. I was stuck in this chair and Beautyful was out doing God knows what with God knows who. Na, I was about to stick to my nickname and cause a mothafucking Chaos.

CHAPTER FOUR
BEAUTYFUL

I listened to my sister boast about her professional football player husband. Something she always does whenever we three get together. I sipped on my mai-tai as I pretended to listen to her stories of life as a footballer's wife.

Toni's and my eyes connected and we made a secret face before we giggled with one another. I mean, I loved my sister and everything, and I was really happy she was married to *the* Dorian Slater. He played as a quarterback for the Philadelphia Hawks. However, the constant reminder of how fabulous her multi-million-dollar life was, got exhausting. I mean it's not as though me and Toni were doing bad ourselves.

Dorian and my sister met when she worked at a high-end restaurant as a waitress. Dorian and a few of his teammates went to have dinner one night after they won their game.

My sister ended up being their waitress that night. Dorian apparently liked what he saw, asked her out, and the next thing you know, she's been married for the last two and a half years with an almost two-year-old daughter named Phoenix.

"Anyway, how are things with DeAndre?" my friend Toni

cut in the middle of Lovely's blabbering. I smiled mischievously at her before I opened my mouth to answer her question.

"Hmm, let me see." I thought about where to begin as I took a sip of my drink. "He's slowly turning into an alcoholic. He barks at me and picks a fight every chance he gets. Oh, and he told me I looked like a prostitute before I left the house tonight." I made a thoughtful face as I tried to recollect if I forgot anything else.

"Damn, I told your ass from jump that a man with a nickname like Chaos would bring nothing but turmoil to your life," Lovely interjected. Taking a long sip of my beverage, I rolled my eyes at her over the rim of my glass.

"Lovely, you know damn good and well Chaos is just going through it right now. Once he comes to terms with his paralysis and acting like a little pussy, he'll be back to loving his wife again. Why you gotta rub shit in her face?" Toni said with a dramatic roll of her eyes.

Toni and my sister rarely saw eye to eye. Which was weird because they were thick as thieves when we were younger. I'm not too certain when things went left with their friendship but they hardly were on the same page.

My sister believed that Toni was jealous of her life. The famous and wealthy husband, the lavish lifestyle and all that. Of course, Toni insisted Lovely's life was anything but perfect and that she was faking it until she made it.

Toni Monet, my thirty-two-year-old friend, was always ready to have my back. I admired her as she sassed my sister with her flawless golden skin, her voluptuous figure that she carried with nothing but grace. I secretly wished I had her curves. She had a pair of full bouncy breasts, long, thick, juicy thighs. Full rounded hips that surrounded a stomach that wasn't flat but hell...she looked good any damn way.

Her hair was in a short curly afro. Reddish brown in color, she had the cutest button nose and a pair of full, pouty lips that were kind of oval shaped. Toni was a divorce lawyer that worked her ass off to get to where she was now. Toni had a couple skeletons in her closet but me and Lovely never made her feel any type of way about it. She was our girl regardless.

Toni wasn't married and if given the chance she probably would never be. My girl was a strong, *I don't need a man, don't want a man, I'm not bringing anything to the table because I am the fucking table type of woman.*

Toni had a son, his name was Aiden. His father, Earon, Toni's fiancé died when he was just one year old in a car accident. That shit was so devastating for Toni, I thought she would have never recovered from that loss. However, she eventually did and her trying to get back into the dating world was like watching somebody repeatedly bump their head against a brick wall. Just brutal because no one was ever good enough!

"Toni, don't you start with me," my sister said, pointing her well-manicured index finger at Toni. I sighed softly, knowing I would have to stop them from going at each other's throat soon. I don't know why Lovely even bothered starting shit with Toni. Especially knowing what she did about our friend.

"Well then don't you go acting like everyone can have the perfect husband with the perfect life like you," Toni mumbled before snatching her strawberry daiquiri and taking a sip. An exaggerated stank look on her pretty face.

"It must be so hard being jealous of me."

Oh no, Lovely did not have to take it there, I thought to myself, palming my face with my right hand.

"Jealous? Bitch, *puhlease*," Toni stressed on her words, rolling her eyes dramatically.

"It's not my fault you can't meet a man because you're so busy trying to be **the man**."

Oh hell no. My sister was doing too much. I made a face at her before putting my glass on the table, ready to tell her off.

"Remind me again who's the female in you and Dorian's marriage. Because the both of y'all *some bitches*." Toni raised her eyebrow, taunting Lovely who was cutting her eyes at my friend.

"Will you two stop it." I held my hand up at the both of them. My eyes darted back and forth between them.

"I don't have time for this, I'm going to use the bathroom real quick." Lovely grabbed her designer purse, rolled her eyes hard at Toni before she got up, and made her way to the restroom area.

"You my girl and everything, but your sister be getting on my nerves." Toni sighed heavily, reaching for the cherry at the bottom of her glass and popping it in her mouth.

"I swear the both of you need to get it together. Shit is fucking annoying," I mumbled, looking around the room. My eyes looked at the bar area and saw a familiar face.

"Hey, isn't that your neighbor from your old apartment?" I asked, tipping my head in the direction my eyes were looking in. Toni turned her attention to where my eyes were and sighed loudly.

"God, I hope she doesn't see me." Toni slid down a little in the chair she was seated in, hoping she would go unnoticed.

I was about to giggle at her silliness when a thought suddenly hit me.

"Wait a minute, does Sabrina still work as a neurological physical therapist at the private institution, Victoria's Medical Services?" I asked Toni as an idea popped into my head.

"Girl, I do not know." She answered with attitude.

"Can you call her over?" Toni made a hell no face at me.

"Come on, please, I need to find another physical therapist for DeAndre. Look, she's walking away," I pointed at Sabrina who had a beer in her hand. She placed it to her lips and took a long gulp as she began walking away. She was sucking on that beer bottle like her name was Samuel instead of Sabrina.

"You lucky I love you," Toni said before releasing an annoyed sigh just before she got up and made her way over to Sabrina. I stuck the tip of my index finger in my mouth, nibbling on my acrylic nail nervously.

I smiled to myself when Toni convinced Sabrina to come over to where I was seated.

"Um, Beautyful, you remember my old neighbor, Sabrina," Toni said. We had met before in the past a couple of times. I waved at her, giving her my winning smile.

Sabrina licked her lips in a seductive manner, eyeing me suggestively. Fun fact, Sabrina was as gay they come, and she definitely never hid it. She used to hit on Toni hard as hell when they were neighbors, which really annoyed Toni because she said Sabrina never took no for an answer.

"How have you been, Beautyful, with your fine ass self?" Sabrina was what would be considered a lipstick lesbian. She was a very pretty female. She would rock the latest frontal wigs and her face card never declined as her makeup skills were crazy.

Toni said Sabrina confessed that having a girl appearance instead of looking like a dyke lesbian made her get females that were willing to experiment with what it would be like to have sex with a woman. Sabrina said that was the best type of chick to get, claiming the sex was better.

"I've been good. I was wondering if you still work as a neurological physical therapist." I didn't hesitate to get straight to the point as I crossed my fingers that were on my lap.

"Yeah, I do. What's up?" Sabrina questioned, taking a sip of her beer.

Cheering in my mind, I sat upright as I looked at Toni's expressionless face. "I need a therapist to work with my husband. He was shot in his back and the bullet damaged a nerve, causing temporary paralysis. Can you suggest someone?" The question jumped off my tongue with anticipation.

"Yeah, there's this new chick that started working a few months ago. I can ask her and get back to you if you'd like," Sabrina replied in a somewhat seductive manner.

"Yes, that would be so great," I told her enthusiastically with a smile on my face.

"Alright, gimme your phone so I can put my number in." Sabrina stretched her hand out, waiting for me to place my cell in her palm. Faster than lightning, I fished my phone out my clutch, unlocked it, and gave it to her.

With a stupid grin on my face, I watched eagerly as she punched her number in before giving me my phone back.

"I'll call you in the next day or two after I have a talk with Keisha. See you later, Toni." She turned her attention to Toni who in return gave her a fake tight smile. Blowing Toni a kiss, Sabrina gave me a wave before she sauntered away.

"Ugghhh, Sabrina thinks she could turn any straight woman into wanting pussy, I swear," Toni said with an exasperated sigh.

"I dunno, I like her. Maybe you should give it a whirl... You reject every nigga that comes your way anyway. Maybe your next relationship is meant to be with a female." I stifled a laugh at the way Toni twisted her face at me.

"Shut the fuck up, Beautyful," she answered in complete annoyance. Her reaction made me laugh even harder.

"Aye, sis." Lovely's presence made me jump a little because

it was like she appeared out of nowhere as she spoke in my ear, a little too loudly.

"Girl, what? You almost buss my damn eardrum," I fussed at her before I stuck my index finger in my ear and wiggled it around.

"You wouldn't believe who I just saw as I was walking back over here," she said while looking over her shoulder repeatedly.

"Who?" I asked, with a crease in my forehead looking around. On God, I was expecting her to say DeAndre done followed my ass at this bar.

"Devon Campbell."

Oh no! I thought, wishing that I could close my eyes, say some magic words, and somehow disappear into thin air.

"Shit, did he see you?" I whispered harshly, afraid all of a sudden to look over my shoulder. Matter of fact, I was so shocked, I didn't even know why in the hell I was even whispering.

"Na, I managed to duck behind a couple people and came back here without being noticed," Lovely answered, pulling her phone out of her handbag as she began texting somebody.

"Oh, girl, you're in trouble...that nigga is still fine," Toni interjected, looking behind me with a smile on her face. I groaned softly before I slowly turned around to see my ex-boyfriend, Devon. I tucked my lower lip in as I studied him unseen.

He was with a very beautiful female, and his hand rested on her lower back as he guided her over to the bar area.

I ogled him shamelessly. He was a tall guy with a slim body type and nice cocoa color. He rocked a low haircut with the sides tapered down and low, well-maintained facial hair.

Devon was the last relationship I had before DeAndre decided to wife me. A pang of hurt hit me when I thought about the way Devon's and mine relationship ended. It was not on the best of terms because I allowed DeAndre to practically steal me from Devon, who was actually a good man.

A nostalgic feeling washed over me as I remembered the way DeAndre practically disappeared from my life after I allowed him to give me the most mind-blowing orgasm with his fingertips at a house party, I didn't want to attend in the first place. Before then I had literally never experienced an orgasm before.

I remember listening to my sister and Toni talk about their sexual encounters and the way their men made them experience toe-curling orgasms. I would participate in the conversation but I would be lying through my teeth. The only way I even achieved an orgasm was when I masturbated...until DeAndre gave me my first that night.

The night at the house party that I attended with Lovely and Toni, when DeAndre told me he would be right back, he did not return. Instead, a series of gunshots rang out causing pure mayhem. Lovely and I began screaming at the top of our lungs. We started running looking for Toni and before I knew it, we ran straight out the house and into Toni's CRV.

I recall wanting to go back to see if DeAndre was alright, not to mention I hadn't given him my phone number that he'd asked for. I seriously thought about shouting to Toni to turn her vehicle around but I stayed quiet. DeAndre knew where I worked so if he really was interested, he would come to my workplace and sweep me off my feet.

Yeah, that never happened! A week turned into two and a month turned into three. DeAndre never showed and he never even called my office phone, which I knew he could have also done.

I felt used and cheap. I allowed him to have his way with me at that party. He probably thought I was some easy hoe that allowed just any random nigga to play with my pussy whenever he liked. I was beyond mortified. As if that wasn't enough, the doctor's office where I worked suddenly had to close when the owners of the building sold it without any kind of notification to the tenants who were renting.

We had no choice but to close our doors permanently when the new owners stated they would be tearing the building down to put up an apartment complex.

Now I had the task of finding a new job and finally I had begun to forget about DeAndre. I chalked up our few encounters to a learning experience and promised to be more careful next time I met a man.

After being unemployed for about a month, I finally landed a job at an office as a administrative assistant. I enjoyed my job for the most part and I especially enjoyed my view of the cubicle directly in front of me.

This nigga was so fine to me. He was tall and slender, he always wore black work pants and pastel-colored shirts. He worked as the payroll clerk and mostly kept to himself. The fact that he barely interacted with his coworkers didn't stop me from looking for petty reasons to talk to him.

"Do you have some staples I can borrow? Can I borrow your glue stick?" were some of the questions I asked, knowing damn well I could get my ass up and go to the stationary cabinet and get my own shit.

Devon was just a breath of fresh air. I finally seemed to have caught his attention at our office farewell party for one of our workers who was migrating to Egypt with her husband. He stayed close to me throughout the get together, asking personal questions about my family life and shit.

Our relationship started off nice and slow. Both Devon and I were guarding our hearts. He had recently gotten out of a bad break-up and didn't want to rush into anything too quickly.

That was totally fine by me because men had a way turning the most level-headed female into a raging lunatic.

A few months passed and I realized how much of an awesome guy Devon was. My father loved him and Lovely thought he was really good for me. There was no doubt in my mind that Devon and I were a great match. He was respectful and told me often how much he appreciated having me in his life. So if he was so wonderful, what could possibly have been the problem?

Unbeknownst to anyone, Devon's and my sex life wasn't so great. If I was being brutally honest, it was downright awful. I tried to look past it and concentrated on the fact that he was such a good guy. However, the more I tried the more I dreaded our next sexual encounter.

If that wasn't embarrassing enough, the one and only time I was able to achieve an orgasm with him was when I pictured DeAndre. How absolutely mortifying that my man was performing oral sex on me and I was faking every moan that passed my lips.

The next thing I knew, DeAndre's face suddenly popped in my head. His sexy ass voice whispered in my ear, *"You got the wettest pussy a nigga ever felt. I bet this shit tastes off the mothafucking chain. I wanna stick my tongue in it."*

Those words he said to me that night at the party sounded off in my head and to my utter disbelief, my body reacted. I began to writhe under Devon's mouth lustfully while I moaned loudly in the process.

"You think you'll like it if I eat this pussy?" Phantom DeAndre asked me once again.

"Ssss, yesss," I moaned loudly, pushing Devon's face into me even more as I spasmed out of control as I came.

That shit could not happen again. I had to get this man out of my head. I could just tell Devon that his bedroom skills did nothing for me. Maybe I should suggest watching porn together and commenting on what looks like fun, hoping he'd learn a couple new moves.

None of those things ever came to pass because I was way too chicken shit. So for the next few months I continued having bad sex and faking the shit out of my orgasms.

About six or seven months into the relationship with Devon, one of our coworkers named Marissa invited just about everyone to her wedding. Devon told me he wanted to attend, but I did not want to go. Marissa was one of my least favorite people at the office. She was so *show-offy*, she had the best body, the best house, the best soon-to-be husband...blah blah.

Her fiancé was very questionable to me. He definitely sold drugs. He would pick her up in practically a new car every damn month. His gold chains, rings, and wristbands were big and plentiful. She claimed he worked at the post office, which was laughable.

Reluctantly, I agreed to attend with Devon. We even color coordinated our outfits. I wore a sweetheart-cut lilac dress that was very short because Devon often told me I had the prettiest toned legs he'd ever seen. He loved when I showed them off. On my feet were a pair of black pumps.

My hair was pulled into a french twist to show off my neck and not-so-expensive necklace and matching earrings set.

Devon wore a pair of black slacks and a lilac vest to match my dress with a white shirt inside. We both complemented one another wonderfully as we sat in the dining hall at Marissa's reception.

Yeah, this nigga is definitely a drug dealer, I thought as I looked around at the questionable faces in attendance. Almost all of the men looked rough and I was certain they had their weapons tucked in their waist.

"Damn, this crowd is different," Devon whispered in my

ear as Marissa and her new husband slow danced to a Luther Vandross song.

"I told you it would be," I answered, and we both laughed softly.

Twenty minutes later and I was sick of being here. I was beginning to realize maybe I was an introvert. Socializing much just didn't do it for me.

"Would you like me to get you something to drink?" Devon asked, eyeing my empty champagne glass.

"Sure, thanks." I turned to him with a smile. He kissed my lips before he got up and headed over to the bar. Sighing softly, I looked around at a few of my coworkers with their significant others.

I decided that when Devon came back, I was about to tell him we should bid farewell to the bride and groom.

My eyes damn near jumped out their sockets as I scanned the room for like the fifth time and saw someone dapping up the groom.

No, it can't be! I shouted in my head before squinting my eyes in disbelief. Oh, but it was.

DeAndre and Marissa's husband stood laughing and talking a few feet from where I sat. I wanted to duck and hide under the table just so we didn't have to see one another.

Tilting my head a little to the right, I eyed the man that practically vanished from my life. It had been almost a year since our ordeal at the house party and I had never heard from nor seen him again.

Yet here he was looking fine as hell. His black slacks showing off his well-kept body, the baby blue Polo long sleeved shirt snuggly hugged his upper body. He seemed slightly bigger in the arms and chest area, maybe he had taken up weight training. From where I sat the tattoos on his neck peeked out from his shirt collar.

His handsome face was surrounded by freshly cut facial hair and his low fade had so many waves the Atlantic Ocean had nothing on him. My heart was beating so loudly behind my ribcage I was sure it was louder than the music played by the DJ.

The butterflies were flying like crazy as I studied him. Then a female appeared next to his side, a half-naked female if I might add. Her dress was cut so low at the back that if she sneezed her ass cheeks would be on display. A strange feeling filled up my insides when DeAndre introduced his female friend to the groom. She giggled like an idiot as she shook his hand.

They say you can feel when someone's eyes are on you. That's the only explanation that I could have come up with when DeAndre suddenly turned and looked straight at me.

His expression changed to that of absolute shock as he just stood there staring at me. Our eyes were locked in. I wished I was strong enough to break the connection he still managed to have over me.

Like a magnetic force somehow drawing us to each other, he shoved his left hand inside of his pants pocket and began to take his first steps toward me.

"They were all out of red wine. The bartender said this was just as good," Devon said, placing the glass in front of me, and then he kissed my neck lovingly before he sat down. Turning to my man, I smiled, thanking him before picking up the glass. As I raised my drink to my lips I allowed my eyes to drift back over to DeAndre. His steps had halted and he had an angry scowl on his face as he eyed Devon.

Nodding his head twice to me, he spun on his heels and walked off, leaving his poor girlfriend confused as she all but ran behind him.

I wished I could say seeing him after all those months

meant nothing to me. I wished I could say the rest of my evening was spent with me and my man enjoying each other's company. Then we went home to have our usual uneventful sex.

I wished that was what happened...but it didn't!

CHAPTER FIVE
BEAUTYFUL

"Aye, don't you hear me talking to you?" My sister shook me a little, bringing me out of my reverie. I looked over at her and blinked repeatedly, drawing myself back to the present.

"I'm sorry...what?" I asked her, clearing my throat, feeling a little embarrassed.

"I said I think that's his wife he's with. She got a big ass rock on her finger," Lovely replied boldly, eyeing Devon and his companion. I smiled a little because he deserved every bit of happiness and more.

"His wife, wow. I'm truly happy for him. He was always such a stand-up guy," I said sincerely.

"Are you sure?" Toni asked with an eyebrow raised. She had a sarcastic look on her face that said I was full of shit.

"Yes, I'm sure. I'm happy he's married." Truth be told, I never told my sister nor my best friend about my lack of sexual appetite when it came to Devon. I also never told them the real reason why our relationship ended. Frankly, they didn't need to know the sordid details.

My breath hitched in my throat when Devon suddenly looked my way. He faltered a bit but only for a split second before he bent and said something to the female he was with. The next thing I knew, he collected their drinks and they walked away without him giving me so much as a second glance.

I couldn't say I was surprised by his reaction. Matter of fact, I fucking deserved his dismissive attitude.

"Damn, that nigga said bye Felicia," Toni cracked.

Choosing to remain silent, I reached for my drink and took a sip as I watched Devon make his retreat.

"You ever gonna tell us the real story behind why y'all two broke up?" Lovely asked.

Not bothering to look her way, I cleared my throat softly.

"We just wanted different things, Lovely," I answered her. By different things I meant I wanted DeAndre's dick and not Devon's.

Toni and Lovely started talking amongst themselves about their kids and my mind drifted back to that night of the wedding.

"I just need to take this call babe, it's Lovely. Let me see what she wants and then I'll be right back." I snatched my phone from off the table before Devon could say anything, smiling sweetly as I stepped in the direction of the entrance.

My phone call merely lasted a few seconds because my sister just wanted the number for my nail tech. Standing outside in the open air alone made me feel like enjoying the night's air a bit longer. Not giving it much thought, I spotted a gazebo in the garden about a two-minute walk away and decided to go toward it.

Loving this quiet spot away from everyone, I sat on a wooden bench in the darkness as I stared at my phone's screen. The only person on my mind was DeAndre. My insides grew warm as I remembered him. The way he looked so incredibly handsome in his suit, and I wasn't sure, but there was something different about him.

His aura, it was stronger somehow. His presence demanded attention as he stood there speaking to Marissa's husband. His suit I could tell was expensive, very expensive. There was a change about him I couldn't explain, but he was a different man.

"Uggh," I expressed my disgust with myself, groaning while rolling my eyes. I was upset that I allowed DeAndre to invade my thoughts the way he did. I needed to get it *to-fucking-gether*. Deciding that I should get back to the reception and try to enjoy the rest of the night with Devon, I got up and prepared to leave.

I saw him the same time I smelled the pungent odor of the cigar he was smoking. I froze immediately at DeAndre who dipped his head back and blew out a thick cloud of white smoke into the cool night's atmosphere.

How did he even know I was out here? *Oh wait, maybe he came out here to smoke and accidentally bumped into me.* It was a little arrogant of me to think he followed me out here, especially when he came with a slut on his arm. I don't even know why I seemed irritated that he was here with someone because so was I.

I wasn't going to say a thing to him. I was just going to brush right past him and be on my way. Besides, he didn't deserve for me to say shit to him after the way he treated me.

With my chin haughtily in the air, I marched to where he stood blocking the entrance with his tall, perfect body. I didn't mean to think his body was perfect, but I already thought it... the damage was done.

"Excuse me," I said to him, refusing to give him eye contact. Instead, I stared at his chest. I waited for him to move out my damn way but instead, he just stood there. His refusal to clear my path gave me no choice but to look up at him.

Fuck, why did I have to look at him? I screamed in my head as our eyes locked.

"Who's that lame ass nigga you with?" he asked me, placing the cigar to his lips as he puffed away.

I twisted my face at him because he sure did have a lot of fucking nerve. I hadn't seen him in damn near a year and he was insulting my man. I was not about to do this with him.

"Can you please move before I knock your ass over?"

Now I was just lying to myself. There was no way I could push DeAndre out of my way since he was way bigger than me. Chuckling under his breath, he planted his feet more firmly in place.

"I would love to see you try," he challenged me.

Releasing a breath of frustration, I looked at him with irritation before I sucked my teeth.

"You play too fucking much. You probably can't even remember my name," I sassed him, putting a hand on my waist. His head jerked back as though I was crazy to suggest such nonsense.

"You never answered my question, *Beautyful*," he pronounced my name in an exaggerated way to prove me wrong. "Who is that you're with?"

I looked to the right of me as I scoffed loudly at him before turning back and giving him my full attention.

"Who do you think you are? You disappear that night at the party and then for the rest of the year up until now. You never even tried to contact me even though you knew exactly where I worked. Now you're standing here demanding answers to a question as though you have some kind of rights over me. You're unbelievable, not to mention you're here with someone also." I shook my head and looked away again, shocked by his audacity.

"Is that what you think, that I never tried to find you? The night at the party I came back to the spot I last saw you at and you and your sister were gone. I looked for you for a few minutes but I guess the gunshots ran y'all off.

"Secondly, I got a call literally two days after and flew out to Colombia for three months on business. A nigga thought about you every day, and every time I did I cursed myself for not getting your number before I went to stop my nigga Bjorn from fighting." DeAndre's explanation made me spin my head back to him. Was he telling the truth? I read people well enough and most times I could pick up on whether they're lying or not.

The look on his face told me he was probably telling me the truth.

"Once I came back from Colombia, I swear on the millions in my bank account, the first thing I did was come by your office. My heart plummeted to the ground when I saw the building had been closed. I even asked a couple people who were walking minding their business if they knew where the doctor's office had moved to, but they didn't know what the hell I was even talking about. I took my phone out and called my momma up and questioned her.

"When she said the doctor had closed up his practice for good, I had no clue where to look. Hell, I even searched you up on Google, tried to pull you up on Facebook...nothing." My face softened at his admission because he had to be telling the truth. I'm not on any social sites because that shit was so negative more than half the time.

Putting his cigar out, he tossed the stub on the ground. "I looked for you, I swear I did, but I literally couldn't find you." He took a step closer to me. "There was never a day that went by that your beautiful face never popped in my head...Beautyful." He stepped even closer so the space between our bodies was now non-existent.

My breathing slowed down significantly, and I knew I should not be entertaining this man. He was nothing but trouble...dangerous even.

"Remember when I told you I will make you my wife and I will be your husband?" he asked, reaching up to gently caress my earlobe. I nodded my head, too lost in the brown pools of his eyes to answer.

"After my three-month absence in Colombia I can make that happen easily for us. I can now give you the world. I can give you the life every woman has always dreamed of and more." I wanted to protest that being a trophy wife was never a dream of mine. I loved working and making my own money.

However, I said nothing. Instead, I held my breath as DeAndre's head dipped slowly toward me. My eyes focused on his lips and I desperately wanted to feel their softness once more. I was going to allow him to kiss me, but only once and then I'd pull away, reminding him that I was in a relationship as was he.

That plan seemed simple enough until I actually felt his lips on mine, and then it went to shit.

Our mouths felt as though they were barely touching as he kissed me. I closed my eyes as the tip of his tongue traced the crease where my lips met, prying them open. I was only happy to oblige by opening my mouth as his tongue snaked its way in.

Melting into his touch as he placed his arms protectively around my body, he drew me into him. Moaning in his mouth, I wrapped my arms around his neck and hungrily kissed him back.

What started off as a gentle and innocent kiss quickly transformed into animalistic behavior.

"Mmm...ow," I said when DeAndre sank his teeth into my lower lip, pulling it gently as he watched my face contort with the pain I felt.

"You still got the wettest pussy?" he asked me as I felt his fingers creep up my thigh, slowly making their way to the outside of my lace thong.

The countless times I fantasized about this moment right here. When I would feel DeAndre's touch bringing my body to life the way Devon never could.

He brushed his lips against my jawline until they were pressed against my ear. I shut my eyes tightly when his middle finger circled my clit, my wetness running down my leg slowly.

"Yeah, you still got that gushy shit. I dreamed of finally being able to taste you. Get this wet ass pussy in my mouth so all your mothafucking juices can run down the back of my throat. And right now I'm thirsty as a mothafucka." DeAndre's words were enough to make me cum on myself right here.

Hiking my dress above my waist, DeAndre pushed me back until I was seated once more inside the gazebo.

This was wrong. I should stop him. I should tell him not to get down on his knees between my thighs. Yeah, I should stop him from yanking my thong underwear to one side. I definitely should not allow him to put his mouth on me as he lowered his head between my legs. My boyfriend was inside, probably wondering where I was.

"Shitttt," I moaned, tipping my head back as I looked at the roof of the gazebo. All of my should haves went out the fucking window when DeAndre's tongue circled my clit with a quickness.

"Grind on my mouth," DeAndre instructed, and I was more than willing to do as I was told. Rocking the lower half of my body in time with his licks, flicks, and sucks, I quickly felt my release building.

"Yeah baby, that's it...cum in my mouth."

"Oh my god," I whispered softly as I stared at the roof of the gazebo. Grabbing the back of DeAndre's head, I got ready to have the most mind-blowing orgasm I swore only he could give me.

"Shit...shit," I cried out as my body convulsed. Lifting my butt off the bench a little, I writhed against his mouth.

"Oh shit!" This time my curse word wasn't that of pleasure, it was that of shock and surprise. Because when I opened my eyes and looked at the gazebo's entrance, Devon was standing there with the most disgusted look on his face.

"Devon...I...this," I stuttered, looking for the correct words to explain why I was getting my pussy ate when I told him I was going to answer my sister's phone call. But really, what explanation could I have given? I would have definitely lost my case in court. All the evidence was right before him.

Saying another man's name and me shoving his head away sure had DeAndre confused by the look on his face as he gazed up at me. Seeing that something had my attention to the back of him, he turned around.

Slowly, he got to his feet as I struggled to cover my exposed lower half. DeAndre dusted off his black pants and casually adjusted his jacket without a care in the whole world. He sauntered over to where Devon was standing.

"Sup, my name is Chaos," DeAndre casually introduced himself to Devon and then licked my juices from his lips with a smirk on his face.

"Alright y'all, my husband texted for the third time tonight. I think it's time I headed home." Lovely's voice was a welcomed interruption because that particular memory made me cross my legs tightly.

Wriggling in my seat because my body was tingling in places I wanted to be touched, I tried to ignore the horniness I felt. Even though DeAndre had been paralyzed from the waist down, his dick still worked just fine. However, the way his feelings were set up at the moment, sex was something we did not have often.

I could count on one hand the amount of times we had sex since the shooting. Of course, I didn't mind climbing on top of my husband and riding him like a horse. Nothing I haven't done a hundred times before the accident. However, DeAndre's ego seemed more damaged than his spinal cord.

He felt emasculated over the fact that he couldn't get on top, turn me around, or hold my legs in the air when we fucked. I tried just about everything to show him just how much he still turned me on and that I still wanted him. Everything I did was in vain though.

His paralysis seemed to open a Pandora's box because having to deal with his crazy ass mood swings, him wanting to drink while on medication truth be told, I was also sex starved. I swear my life couldn't get any fucking worse.

"Ok, sis, I gue—" the remainder of my sentence got lost in my throat when I looked at Bjorn's tall ass walking over to our table.

"I know you fucking lying," I mumbled under my breath as my jaw loosely hung open.

"Oh shit, your nigga done sent a stalker 'cause he couldn't stalk you himself," Lovely cracked. Apparently, she forgot she was just leaving because she made no move to get up from her seat.

"Hello ladies," Bjorn's husky voice greeted us. He spoke to all of us but his eyes never left my sister's face. Ever since Jesus was a baby, this nigga had been crushing on my sister. I always suspected he liked her and often asked DeAndre to clarify if my suspicions were correct.

He would always shrug his shoulders and tell me to mind my business. It was only when my sister was about to get married Bjorn questioned me about why she liked Dorian and finally admitted that he had a thing for Lovely. He waited until she was about to walk down the aisle to confess how he felt. Men surely did suck when it came to expressing their feelings.

Lovely, on the other hand, I had no clue if she even saw the signs that Bjorn was into her. I was almost 100% certain she wouldn't be into him though. Her choice in men was usually the uptight, goody two shoes type. My sister and I were really different.

Shoving my hands inside my jeans pocket, I sulked at Bjorn. "Let me holla at you over by the bar," I told him, leading the way so I could give him a piece of my mind.

"What the hell are you doing? I know you did not let DeAndre bamboozle you with his bullshit and convince you to come down here and spy on me," I immediately went in on Bjorn as I folded my arms angrily under my breasts.

"You know the real reason why I came," he answered, peering over my shoulder at my sister. Rolling my eyes, I shook my head at him.

"Bjorn, Lovely is a *happily* married woman. You took too damn long to say how you feel about her," I told him, releasing a frustrated sigh, rubbing my forehead.

"Yeah, how can you be so sure that she's happily married? You're just assuming shit. Her marriage isn't gonna last. Anyway, why you left the house dressed like a prostitute?" Bjorn joked, chuckling under his breath looking at my outfit before he shook his head a little. I groaned loudly because that was probably what DeAndre told him to get him to come down here. That I left the house looking like an escort.

"Please, with that prostitute bullshit. If I didn't get out of that fucking house I was going to commit murder. I don't know how much more I can take of Chaos and his *pity party nonsense*." I exhaled loudly and looked over at Lovely who was gathering her shit getting ready to leave.

"I mean, you know he didn't mean to say that to you. I see you trying and I wish he could see that too. Just give him some time, maybe his next physical therapist will be the one to really turn shit around." Bjorn tried his best to comfort me.

Over the past three months since the shooting, Bjorn had been nothing but nice to me. He always spoke nothing but positivity to me, encouraging me not to give up on my husband. Honestly, I thought he was trying to ensure I wouldn't leave DeAndre's ass.

Deciding I won't mention to him that I spoke to someone about a new therapist because I thought I'd jinx it, I simply shrugged my shoulders at what he said.

"Let me go say bye to Lovely, she's about to leave." Not waiting for him to respond to what I said, I turned and walked back to our table.

"I'm sorry, I gotta go. Dorian has practice. Come here and give your big sis a hug." She turned to me with her arms open. I practically fell into her arms because a hug was just what I needed. We embraced each other tightly. Whispering that everything will work out in God's time in my ear, Lovely pulled away.

She got somewhat of a nervous look on her face as she turned to Bjorn, who came to stand next to me.

"It was nice seeing you, Bjorn," she said with a tight smile before turning to Toni. "I love you girl, even though we can never get along half the time for some reason."

Lovely and Toni laughed before they quickly hugged one

another and she turned to leave. I was about to tell Bjorn to put his tongue back in his mouth before my phone started ringing.

My Love popped up on the screen and I groaned to myself. Saying a quick prayer before I swiped the screen to answer DeAndre's call.

"Yes, De—"

"The fuck your ex doing in the same spot where you're at? You arranged to meet up with that nigga! Are Lovely and Toni even there with you?" DeAndre barked at me from the other end. Shocked that he even knew about Devon, I turned to Bjorn. He had to be the one to mention this to him.

"What? Ho-how do you even know that? Besides, we don't even speak anymore. You of all people should know that, Chaos." I was so sick and tired of always trying to deal with his bi-polar ass mood swings.

"Bring your ass home!" he screamed before he hung up on me.

"What did you say to him?" I asked Bjorn in an accusing manner with an angry look on my face.

"The fuck you mean? I haven't spoken to that nigga since I left y'all house."

The back of my eyeballs stung because at this point, I was so overcome with emotion I was about to burst into tears in this sports bar. I turned to Toni who was already on her feet.

"I'm sor—"

"It's ok, I understand. Go deal with your husband. I was ready to leave anyway." She hugged me and then squeezed my shoulders. Smiling, Toni told me again to go home to my husband and that she would be fine.

"Call me when you get home alright," I told her, and she nodded in agreement.

Cutting my eyes at Bjorn, I snatched my clutch from off the table and turned to leave.

"On God, I didn't say anything, Beautyful," Bjorn repeated, but I paid him no mind. I was so sick of everyone and their shit. My phone began ringing again in my hand. Looking at the phone as I made my way to my car in parking lot, *My Love* was on the screen.

"Fuck you, Chaos. Fuck you," I said, refusing to answer his call as I unlocked the door and hopped in behind my steering wheel.

Once I sat down, happy to have some privacy, I grabbed the steering wheel with both my hands, shut my eyes tightly, and released a blood-curdling scream.

CHAPTER SIX
LOVELY

Stretching lazily in my huge custom-made king-sized bed, I reached for my husband. My palm fell onto a cool empty spot next to me. Realizing that Dorian was not lying on our bed, I cracked my eyes open one at a time. Groaning at the light that peeked through the blinds, directly hitting me in my face, I covered my eyes with my hands.

"Jesus," I mumbled, feeling the throbbing at my temples letting me know that I shouldn't have drunk more than one mai-tai last night. Sighing loudly, I reached under my pillow for my cell and saw that it was 6:30 a.m.

Sitting upright, I looked around my spacious bedroom and wondered where my husband was. I was so sprung out of my mind last night that I knocked right out when I got home. The last thing I remembered was walking through the front door, and my husband telling me that the kids were asleep and I shouldn't wait up for him because practice may run late.

Rubbing my eyes, I looked at my phone again and realized that I had a text. Quickly going to my messages, thinking maybe Dorian had texted while I slept, I saw the message came from a number not stored in my phone. I recognized the number immediately and began gnawing at my lower lip, contemplating if I should risk opening his text.

Scanning the room again as though I expected my husband to suddenly appear, I clicked on the message and opened it.

You looked so good tonight...I miss you.

A pang of guilt quickly kicked me in my gut and I deleted the message.

"Fuck," I muttered, wishing that I didn't have feelings for him also, but I did, and for that my guilt was tremendous. Nobody knew about Bjorn's and mine little secret, especially not my sister, and I planned on keeping it that way.

"Mummy!" The excited sound of my daughter calling out to me almost made me jump out of my skin with surprise. Dropping my phone next to me with a startled expression, I giggled as she excitedly jumped on the bed, wrapping her little arms around my neck.

"Oh my goodness," I said, falling back on the sheets as she giggled uncontrollably. I began raining kisses on her face, making her scream even louder.

"Are you hungry?" I asked, tickling her tummy.

"Yesh," she answered the best a two-year-old could.

"Ok, then let's go brush our teeth so I can make my Phoenix-Poo some breakfast." I grabbed her and hopped off the bed with her in my arms.

Fifteen minutes later I had my daughter in her highchair with her Minnie Mouse plate filled with scrambled eggs, pieces of apple, and a few grapes. She ate happily as she watched Dora on the TV.

As I sipped my coffee, smiling as I watched my daughter, a frown slowly formed on my face as I thought about my husband. I had no clue if he was even home or not. Usually if he got in late from practice, he would go sleep in one of the guest bedrooms upstairs. Looking over at Phoenix, she had eaten her fruits and just had the eggs left, so I decided to go in search of Dorian.

"Hey, Momma will be right back, ok my love," I told her, planting a kiss in the middle of her forehead. Phoenix was so engrossed in whatever the hell Dora was looking for she didn't pay any attention to me.

With quick steps I made my way back up the stairs, knowing I couldn't leave Phoenix alone for too long. Slowly inching up to the guest bedroom door where I knew Dorian slept in sometimes, I slowly opened it.

Leaning on the frame of the door as I held on to the handle, I studied my snoring husband. The sheets were wrapped around his naked body because he always slept nude. His defined muscles flinched a little as he breathed in a peaceful rhythm. In the middle of his back was the number eleven, which signified the number he wore on his jersey when he played football.

His caramel complexion glistened and glowed as he slept on his stomach, hugging a pillow tightly. Curling my lips in, I scanned his cornrow hair that was surprisingly very neat after a night of practice. Most times once practice was over his hair would be a hot ass mess from him sweating during his training session.

Placing the steaming caffeine to my lips, I took a sip as I recalled what I said to Toni last night. Accusing her of being jealous of my life. I snorted a little because I was such a fucking faker. My life wasn't anything to be jealous of.

I mean, I was absolutely grateful and all to have met a man like Dorian. It's not every day a simple girl like me meets a wealthy, successful football player who wants me to be a part of his life. I was introduced to the finer things in life when I met my husband.

Dorian and I fell for each other hard. Sometimes I had to pinch myself during the time we were dating, because it was so hard to believe this was my life. The extravagant dates, being showered with expensive gifts and lavish trips. I could not believe my luck.

We weren't dating for a long time before he got down on his knee and proposed. I can't even lie. I definitely felt overwhelmed and thought being with a man for just five months was too short to even think about marriage. Yet, here we were almost three years later, married with a two-year-old.

So, why wasn't I happy? Why did it feel as though I was faking my happy lifestyle to my family and friends? The answer was lying on that bed as he snored a little. I knew Dorian was a good husband and a wonderful father, but sometimes I wished he would be more assertive.

Toni didn't tell one fucking lie when she asked who wore the pants in my marriage. Dorian could never be described as an Alpha male. He just kind of went along with whatever I said and wanted. Some women may have liked that and preferred a docile man like Dorian, but not me. I loved a man's man, one who stepped up and took charge.

Dorian, on the other hand, would always look at me to make a lot of the decisions in the household, in our relationship, even with our daughter. Everything always fell on my shoulders. Like why in the fuck did I even have a husband if I had to make all of the fucking decisions around here?

Then, there was the other thing...our sex life. I wouldn't say our sex was bad, but then again, I wouldn't call it the best either.

Let's just say it was predictable. The lukewarm kisses, the mediocre foreplay, and the one position during our lovemaking, I knew what to expect before Dorian and I even began fucking. One thing I could count on, thank God, was the fact that he could eat pussy like a fucking monster. I was sure to have an orgasm from his mouth. Other than that, his sex wasn't something I looked forward to.

Shaking my head a little to erase the thought that shouldn't have entered my head in the first place, I stepped inside of the room. With very light steps I crept closer to the bed and sat down gently.

Admiring his well-toned body, I smiled, and then a slight frown creased my forehead. Reaching for the small scratch on his right shoulder, I used the tip of my index finger to trace the mark.

Narrowing my eyes to the back of my husband's cornrows, I suddenly felt the urge to pop him upside his head. Taking a couple quick calming breaths, I had to tell myself not to jump to conclusions.

However, there has been something off about my husband that I've noticed over the past few months. It was not just one thing but a couple of things that had me looking at him sideways.

Number one, his practice sessions had been more frequent over the past few months. This wasn't very odd except it was off-season. Dorian claimed their coach wanted them to try some new techniques, so when games resumed everyone will bring their best A game.

I pushed it to the back of my mind, but when Dorian returned to our home he would almost always sleep in the guest bedroom, claiming he came home too late and didn't want to wake me because he knew I was a light sleeper.

I did tell him numerous times that I would prefer and didn't mind if climbed back into our bed no matter the time. However, he only did it twice and because I did wake up on both occasions, he stopped. Ok, I let that slide also, but I did notice whenever he came back from practice his hair would have the appearance of having no sweat. Before he returned home his cornrows would usually be messy, and at least one would be completely undone.

Strands would practically be sticking out all over the place and the next day he would give his hairstylist/barber a call and he would come to our home and re-do his hair. Lately, this was not the case because he came back with his hair neat to the point that he didn't need his cornrows redone. Some people may think I was overreacting, but I knew my husband's routines.

The last thing was what I was looking at right now. The scratches on his back. Dorian would get some sort of bruise during practice, which wasn't unusual, but over the last few months the scratches would be on questionable areas on his body. Places where he would not normally have bruising. Like his shoulder, his lower back, there was even a time I saw a couple on his ass.

I bit into my lower lip as I thought about if it was possible that my fears had finally come through. Dorian was a handsome man, not to mention very wealthy. Any woman would want him for themselves. I would grind my jaw at the way women would flirt with him right in front of my eyes whenever we were out. They would do it in such a disrespectful manner because I would be right there and they would flirt with him shamelessly. Dorian would sense my unease and would reassure me that I was his favorite girl in the world next to our daughter, of course.

I'd never worried about Dorian cheating on me simply because there had never been a reason to after these years. Now, I wasn't so sure. I guess he felt me touching his scratch because he stirred in his sleep.

Pulling back my hand, I smiled a little when he woke up, fully opening his eyes, looking right at me.

"Hey you." He smiled, reaching for me. Dorian rubbed my exposed upper thigh before pushing himself up in a seated position.

"I've told you a million times, no matter what time you get back from practice, come to bed. I don't care if you wake me." I reached for one of his braids and playfully yanked it as I spoke.

"I was coming to lay with you but you were hogging the entire bed with your drunk ass. You were sprawled out on that mothafucka," he chuckled, reaching for the coffee in my hand. I made a face at what he said while he sipped the caffeine.

"Be for real right now. How in the hell can I hog a custom-made king-sized bed?" I made a stank face because he was really trying it.

"That's the same thing I said." Shaking his head, he handed me my cup back as he rolled himself out of bed. I paid close attention as he grimaced in pain before he stood to his feet. Ok, so maybe I was tripping and he did have practice. I wasn't even sure at this point.

Sighing softly, I watched in silence as he walked his toned, muscled, naked body toward the guest bathroom door.

"Where's Phoenix?" he asked without turning around.

Hearing his question made me pounce to my feet because I definitely had left her alone for too long.

"Shit, she's probably done tossed all of her breakfast on the floor by now in protest of being left alone for so long. I'll see you downstairs, babe," I told him as I headed out the bedroom door.

My steps were quick as I drank the last of my coffee. Just as expected, there were eggs on the floor and my daughter sat staring at the television like she didn't just do some Tasmanian devil shit.

"Really Phoenix?" I huffed, looking over at her. She really had all the nerve to make a face at me like she didn't do anything. Walking back to the kitchen to grab some paper towels, I paused when I saw I had a text on my phone that sat on top of the kitchen counter. Picking up my phone, my heart skipped a series of beats when I recognized the number.

I'm not even trippin' on you not responding. You gone belong to me one day.

My heart began to thump once again in my ribcage and I deleted the message. Clutching the edge of the counter, I took a couple deep breaths to calm my nerves. Bjorn was not going to do this to me. He knew I loved my husband no matter what happened between us in the past. I was not going to let temptation get the better of me again.

Snatching a few towels from the roll, I marched back into the living room to clean up my daughter's mess. My family was important to me and I wasn't going to let anyone fuck that up for me.

CHAPTER SEVEN
CHAOS

I cracked my eyes open and immediately knew that something was wrong. Turning my head to the left, I saw that the space next to me was empty. Groaning loudly, I rubbed the overgrown hair on my face.

This was the third morning I had woken up without my wife next to me. Since the night Beautyful came home from being out with her sister and their friend Toni, she hadn't climbed into my bed in the middle of the night.

Exhaling loudly through my mouth, I began feeling like maybe I was a little too hard on her when she came home. Raising my eyes, I looked up at the ceiling and draped my hand on top of my forehead. I thought of the things I said to her that night, wondering what differently I should have said and done.

From the moment I heard the front door open, I wheeled myself into the living room from the kitchen faster than a mothafucka. Eyeing her in disgust as she cut her eyes at me, equally disgusted no doubt on the way I spoke to her over the phone. She tried to get by and walk up the stairs, but I shouted out to her.

"Don't even think to go up those fucking stairs and not explain yourself!"

Pausing immediately with her right foot on the first step and her left planted flat on the ground, Beautyful didn't even bother to turn to me.

"What do you want, Chaos?" she asked, and I could tell her jaw was clenched by the way she sounded.

"What I want is to know why the fuck you left this mothafucka to go kick it with your lame ass ex!" I demanded, wheeling my chair next to where she was standing.

Looking at her right hand, I could see she was gripping the post on the staircase so tightly that her knuckles were turning white. Slowly, Beautyful turned her head to face me, and nothing but repugnance shadowed her pretty facial features.

"Who do you think you are? Sending Bjorn to spy on me as if I'm some badly-behaved teenage girl," she said, shaking her head in disbelief. Tugging on the overgrown hair on my chin, I didn't reply to her accusation because she was wrong.

Bjorn wasn't the one that told me her ex was there. I had eyes everywhere. One of my niggas from back in the day who I still talk to texted me with the info. He knew Devon because of the wedding we attended years ago when Beautyful and I paths crossed again. That night when I got caught with her pussy in my mouth, her nigga threw the first punch after I introduced myself. Let's just say I shut that wedding down with a brawl.

"You think Bjorn's the only nigga I know that could tell me that you're stepping out on me? I have eyes in places you'll never know," I spoke slowly while I purposely looked her up and down in contempt.

Removing her hand from the staircase, taking her right foot off the first step, Beautyful walked over to my chair. I could tell she was angry by the way she was clenching her jaw.

I was ready for the shit storm she was about to unleash on my ass.

"Stepping out on you?" she began, narrowing her eyes at me. "I love you more than I love myself at times, which is bullshit. I have been nothing but supportive of you since your accident. Hell, even before you ended up in that chair I've been your one-woman cheerleader. I've been busting my ass trying to motivate you to get your fucking ass from up off that chair! Your paralysis is temporary, Chaos!

"And the one time I decided to go out and clear my head for a couple hours, you accuse me of cheating on you. All I get is yelled at, spoken to in a derogatory manner, when all I'm trying to do is help your sorry ass. I am sick and tired of you, Chaos!" Beautyful lowered herself to my level so that she was now face to face to me. Both her hands were on the handles of either side of my wheelchair. Glaring at me so hard I was surprised I didn't turn into stone.

"You know what, Chaos? Maybe I should have really cheated on your ass."

Her disrespectful words almost made me lift my hand and slap the taste out of her mouth. Just as I was about to snatch the shit out of her throat and squeeze the fuck out of it, she moved away from me with a quickness.

"Yeah, I see you, you wanna argue some more. Or no, wait, you probably wanna smack the shit out of me, right? Come on then, Chaos. Get your ass out that chair, use the stairlift, and come argue with me some more. We all know arguing is your favorite past time these days," Beautyful taunted me as she began to slowly walk up the stairs backward so she could keep her eyes on me to see if I was about to do what she asked. I have never hit my wife the thought never even crossed my mind...until now. I was that angry.

"Come on Chaos, you think I'm a cheater? You think that I

left this house to go fuck my ex? Let's see you get mad enough to get your sorry ass out that chair and come fuck me up!" Her words had my chest heaving with rage and I clenched my jaw repeatedly. I never felt the need to kill my wife as I did right at this fucking moment.

Now at the top of the stairs, Beautyful folded her arms under breasts. Looking fine as hell in her thigh-high boots as she waited for me to climb out my chair and use the stairlift so I could deal with her disrespectful ass mouth.

"You coming, nigga?" she asked with her head tilted to her left.

Angrily, I huffed my chest before looking at the stairlift, knowing full well I would not use it. Casting my rage-filled eyes at my wife to the top of the stairs, I opened my mouth to spew my loathing at her.

"Fuck you!" I bellowed with hate. I could tell my words had an effect by the way her expression changed. Even from way down at the bottom of the staircase, I could see her eyes grew misty with tears. Slowly, I was turning into a man I no longer recognized. If I was being truthful to myself, I had turned into a man I should not be proud of.

"Yeah, that's what I thought," she said softly before she spun on her heels and walked away.

Pinching the bridge of my nose, I erased the memory from out of mind as I continued laying bed. Ever since that night, my wife hadn't climbed into bed with me, and I must admit...I missed her body. I missed finding her pressed up against me with her head resting comfortably on my chest while she snored soundly.

Another memory played out in my mind at the moment when I started missing her presence. The first time we had sex, which was on the night of the wedding. The night I never believed would happen because I thought I had lost her forever after I got back from Colombia. Me and her ex got into a fist fight after I introduced myself to him.

All I did was stretch my hand out to shake his. It wasn't my fault his girlfriend's juices were still on my lips and I licked it off, which caused him to get mad because he believed that I was taunting him.

The first punch caught me off guard and made me lose my balance, which I quickly regained. I tackled him straight into the garden, destroying his face with my fists. Beautyful was trying her best to stop me from killing her nigga but once I get started, stopping was impossible.

I vaguely remember her running off to get help, which ironically was the very same nigga that told me he saw her ex at the sports bar she was at. He managed to pull me off Devon who was a bloodied mess. His eyes could barely even open by the time I was done.

Beautyful bent to render assistance to him and he mumbled from behind his swollen mouth that she should never touch him and for the rest of her life to never ever speak to him again.

Grabbing her hand, I left the wedding with her, not caring that we both attended with other people. Shawty who accompanied me was pissed to see me leaving with another female.

Beautyful was reluctant as I led her to where I was parked. She tried to free herself from my grasp, but I held her firmly. There was no way I was about to lose her again. I didn't care what I had to do. That night I drove her to my newly purchased home. This was what my trip to Colombia was able to get me. A lavish mansion with multiple bedrooms and bathrooms. A pool both inside and outside, a movie theater, and a gym.

I felt like Tony Montana at times when I stood on my staircase and looked down at my extravagant living space. Puffing my cigar while I admired my sprawling home.

I led Beautyful to my spacious living room. The furnishings were masculine. Everything was leather and black in color. I sat her ass down and began spitting game. Only I really meant what I was saying to her. I wanted her to know that I would like to share my world with her. I wanted to be her everything, I wanted to give her everything, and all she had to do was sit back and allow me to do so.

We sat and talked for the entire night. She shared her family history with me, the fact that her mother passed from kidney failure when she was twenty. Her close relationship with her father because he ended up being a single parent to her and Lovely.

I was floored when she said she never been to a waffle house and I promised I would take her.

She finally shared with me how they came to get the names Lovely and Beautyful. I loved the history lesson of how they were named. Whenever I hear that song "Lovely Day" from now on I'll always think of her.

I could tell she was a headstrong type of female that didn't know how to allow a man to lead. She fought me when I told her I preferred my woman to sit back and let me take care of her. Explaining that she always made a way for herself and didn't feel comfortable letting a man call all the shots.

Beautyful didn't understand the kind of nigga I was. I was the determined type and whatever I wanted, whatever I set my mind to, you better believe that's what I would get. I didn't care what I had to do.

However, she was being stubborn with me. So what my words couldn't convince her to do, I allowed my lips, tongue, and dick to handle the rest. Before she knew what was happening, my tongue was down her throat as my hand crept toward the outside of her underwear.

Her body was so responsive to mine. I didn't hesitate to

shove her dress up once more and put my mouth on her. The way she moaned loudly when my tongue circled her clit. Her moans quickly turned to surprised screams when the pad of my thumb circled her asshole. She came then, in my mouth, panting and calling out my name. Clawing at my back, digging her nails into my flesh.

She just about lost her shit when I went upstairs and came back with a vibrator. Other men felt intimidated to use toys in the bedroom, not me though; that shit was sexy to me. By the time I was done she was agreeing to all of my terms and conditions.

"Fuck," I grunted in even more frustration because the memory had made my dick hard inside my boxers. Looking down at my nine inches standing at attention, I cursed again.

I should be grateful my paralysis only affected my legs and my dick could still do what the good Lord intended it to do. Sex was something I wanted, but I'd be damned if I'll let my wife climb on top of me every time to do the fucking. Shit was emasculating as fuck. As much as I desired my wife I felt embarrassed to initiate being intimate with her.

I missed the way I would twist and turn my her body in all sorts of positions. The fuck I looked like just lying in one spot while she rode me. I preferred to wait until I was back to being 100% again. Even though it sounded selfish, because my wife had needs also, I just couldn't bring myself to getting fucked instead of giving it.

Reaching down, I rubbed my erection through my boxers, wondering if I should buss one off. A soft knock came at the door and I turned my head just as the door was pushed open. Beautyful's head peeped in before she walked slowly into the guest room.

"Good morning," she mumbled, avoiding eye contact with me as she walked over to my bed. Before our blow up she would always help me every morning out of bed, assisting me into my chair. Then she would wheel me inside of the bathroom so I could handle my hygiene. However, since I accused her of leaving our home to cheat on me, she stayed away for the past few days and I had to do the shit myself.

"Morning," I answered, perking up a little because I was genuinely happy to see her. Keeping her face void of any expression, she marched over to the bed. My hand was still on my dick, so when she pulled back the covers my hard-on damn near poked her eyes out.

Curling her lips in, she eyed me suspiciously. "Well, I do hope you got that, because you need to pee. Come on, let me help you up."

Usually when she did this, I would find something to bitch about. I would complain about where she was putting her hands to help or that I simply didn't feel like getting out of bed just yet. This morning, however, I decided to shut the fuck up and let my wife do her thing.

Grabbing my chair, she wheeled it closer to the bed before she helped me in a seated position. Her closeness made me admire her beauty, not to mention she smelled good too. She wore a simple pair of baby blue shorts with a white tank top, and I could tell she was wearing a lacy bra because her nipples imprinted on the front of her top.

Seeing how she was doing her utmost best to avoid eye contact with me, it was safe to say she was still upset.

"Ok, you ready? I'm about to help you get in your chair, take you to the bathroom to see about your hygiene, and then we're going outside to meet somebody," she explained before making a grunting sound as she dragged me over to the chair. I helped her as much as my body allowed me to.

I frowned slightly as she bent and adjusted my feet on top of the footrest.

"To meet who? Who's out there?" My cold and rough demeanor quickly came back as I mean mugged her.

Saying nothing, she released the brakes and began wheeling me toward the bathroom door. Rolling me in front of the sink, she did the simple task of coating the bristles of my toothbrush with toothpaste.

I made no attempt to take it from her outstretched hand, giving her no choice as she finally looked at me.

"Chaos, please. Do not start this mess. Let's just do this, so I can take you outside and meet the person that's willing to work with you. You done chased off so many physical therapists I'm thinking they black balled your name. Please, I don't wanna fight," she explained and shoved the toothbrush closer to me once again.

I really wanted to act petty again. Like I legit just wanted to curse my wife out for getting yet another therapist. It was very obvious none of them knew what they were doing or I wouldn't still be in this damn chair.

However, for the sake of Beautyful and the fact that I was kind of in a good mood this morning, I decided not to stir the pot. Huffing loudly, I took the toothbrush and got to work as my wife stood by.

Twenty-five minutes later I was dressed in a pair of black sweatpants and white Polo t-shirt. Beautyful stood before me with her hand on her chin, looking me over. She eventually got a disapproving expression and I knew she was about to complain about something.

"Are you ready for me to call your barber up? You got a little Wolverine thing going on there." She used her index finger, twirling it around to emphasize her words about my unruly hair and beard.

"I'm not ready yet. Why are you being so nice to me? You left me alone for the last three days." I interlocked my fingers on my lap, waiting for her answer.

With a thoughtful look, her facial features softened and she sighed softly.

"How can you even ask me that? You really believe that I'll just give up on you? I'm still your wife, even though I did contemplate wheeling your ass into the bathroom and dumping you in the tub. Just like my girl did Charles in *Diary of a Mad Black Woman*," she joked before getting behind me to take a hold of the handles on the wheelchair.

Choosing silence, I decided that being quiet was the best thing for the both of us. I knew my wife was probably sick of me and all the bullshit I put her through. So I allowed her to wheel me out of the bedroom toward the living room without fussing. From the moment we entered the room my eyes fell on a female that was dressed in blue scrubs. Her back was facing us, giving me a view of her very curvaceous body and her big, juicy ass.

She had long curly hair that stopped just above her butt. Before she could turn around because she heard us approaching, I just knew she was going to be pretty in the face.

"Keisha, I apologize I took so long," my wife said, bringing me right up to the drop-dead gorgeous female. Looking down at me, she gave me the warmest smile and a dimple made a dent in her right cheek.

Just as I thought, she was fucking stunning. She had flawless, blemish free, pecan-colored skin. Big, bright brown eyes that twinkled when she looked at me. She had the most perfect pair of pink lips.

God damn! I was lusting behind this woman as though my wife wasn't standing two feet away.

"DeAndre, this is Keisha Knowles. Keisha, this is my husband DeAndre," Beautyful introduced us, and I had to remind myself to play it cool. Keisha's smile widened as she held her hand out to me.

"It's a pleasure to meet you, DeAndre. Your wife has told me so much about you. Only good things, I promise," she added with a little giggle.

Her voice was like warm honey I wanted to lick off a spoon.

Fuck! What's the matter with me?

"Nice to meet you." I stretched and took her hand in greeting. My large hand easily enveloped her little fingers. I dismissed the electric jolt I swore I felt when we shook hands.

"Ok, so your wife filled me in on your accident and what's been happening. She said you refused to keep going to therapy at the hospital, which made her acquire home-care workers. I've heard you may not be responding as you should to the therapists hired to work with you in the past.

"There are different stages of paralysis and what you have been experiencing is anger toward your situation. This is the first thing we'll be working on. Once you come to terms with the fact that your legs no longer work like they did before, then and only then will you be able to move forward on the road to recovery."

Keisha sure did say a mouthful, nothing the other therapists hadn't said. I'd heard it all before and I was still in this chair with overcooked spaghetti for legs.

"Yeah, I hear you," I responded in a sarcastic tone. I caught sight of my wife's face. Her eyes were pleading with me to be nice, those eyes were asking me to at least try. Grinding my jaw, I decided to swallow the anger and resentment I had for my situation. I looked at Keisha and opened my mouth to ask a question.

"When can we start?" Beautyful asked before she turned to the lady that was hired to help me walk again.

"Can we do as discussed over the phone and you can start

today?" I could tell she held her breath when she asked that question, awaiting Keisha's response.

"Sure, I have no problem starting today," Keisha answered with a warm smile, her eyes never leaving mine. As she studied me, a strange feeling washed over me and I studied her closer. There was something about this woman I couldn't put my finger on.

I had no idea what I was feeling at the moment, but cheating on my wife was something that I had never done. Matter of fact, it never even crossed my mind because I always felt like my bitch was bad as fuck. Why would I cheat on the baddest bitch? That just didn't make sense to me.

Seated here waiting for this female to begin our therapy session, I felt conflicted. The feeling I felt at this moment, was it attraction? Was I attracted to this bitch that I had to spend the next few months with?

If that was the case, then I was about to be in some serious mothafucking trouble.

CHAPTER EIGHT
BEAUTYFUL

Even though I had been upset with my husband over the past few days, when I received the call from Sabrina this morning, telling me she thinks she found a nurse that can help me, I immediately jumped at the chance because being mad with my husband was one thing. However, he was still my better half and I needed to be there for him. So if I had to get 100 therapists to work with him until I found the right one, then that's what I'd do.

I walked ahead of Chaos, who was being wheeled by Keisha into the gym that I had transformed to his therapy room. There was a table for him to lay on so he could get massages on his back and legs. There were these rail-type things I had to get installed side by side that Chaos had to hold on to as he attempted to walk on his own. The treadmill that had always been here was also supposed to assist him when he finally got back the use of his legs. Other therapists that tried working with him in the past said the treadmill would be used to strengthen his legs.

"Ok, so this is the gym slash therapy room I told you about," I announced, opening the door and switching the light on, illuminating the vast space. I used my hand to point out everything that sat in the space without saying anything while Keisha's eyes bounced off all the equipment.

"This will work perfectly, Beautyful. Are you ready Mr. Pereira?" Keisha asked in a chirpy tone, turning to my husband who had the most unenthusiastic look on his face. I screamed in my head, hoping that he would finally cooperate this time.

"I guess," he answered before setting his eyes on me.

"Ok, in an hour's time you can come in to check on our progress," she said, meaning I needed to get the fuck out her way so she could begin her very expensive one-hour therapy session with my husband.

For a fleeting second, I felt as though I needed to stay and witness what was about to be done. I wanted to sit right on the exercise bike and watch everything she was about to do. I knew I couldn't because just like the other therapists that quit, Keisha explained beforehand that patients worked better without their loved ones in the room. It was said that it gave them a sense of added pressure to make their partner happy and all that did was add unwanted stress. Which eventually would slow down their progress.

"Right, so I'll leave you two and hope that my hard-headed husband will work with you without any issues." I gave Chaos the eye like a mother trying to calm her badly behaved child in a grocery store.

With barely any expression on his face, I rolled my eyes at him before turning to Keisha. Giving her a slight smile, I told her I'd be in the kitchen if she needed me. Then I turned and left the room, closing the door behind me.

Sighing loudly, my steps were quick as I marched to the

kitchen. With the ingredients in my memory, I started taking out what was needed for the pizza dough. Mixing the necessary ingredients in a bowl, I grabbed the rolling pin and began flattening the dough in a circle shape to try a new pizza recipe I thought about.

My mind was all over the place, just racing with random thoughts as I paused to flour the dough. Exhaling softly, I placed the rolling pin down so that I could head over to the refrigerator to grab my tumbler cup. Hopping on top of the granite countertop of the island, I took a sip of my wine.

With my free hand, I massaged my temples and wondered if I made a mistake, asking Keisha to come here. I allowed my mind to go back to this morning as I laid in mine and Chaos's bed upstairs, unable to sleep for like the third night in a row. The saying you sleep better next to the one you love was indeed true. I proved that quote right ever since he got shot and refused to come up to our bedroom.

I would toss and turn, begging Mr. Sandman to pay me a visit, but that nigga never came. It was only when I decided I had no choice, I had to go crawl in bed with my husband downstairs, did that nigga come and blew his sleepy dust in my eyes sending me off to dreamland.

However, I could not bear to even be in the same room with Chaos, much less to share his bed. His actions had been inexcusable and the mere sight of him would send my heart racing. I had been gladly keeping my distance for the last three days.

There were times when I actually got up in the middle of the night and began making my way downstairs to his bedroom. However, I would have a change of heart before I even got to the bottom of the stairs, turn around and climb back under my covers, hoping I would eventually fall to sleep.

I believed that he would have given in and called out for

me to help him out of bed to take him so he could deal with his hygiene. I knew my husband was as stubborn as they came, so he never did.

I actually ended up being low-key impressed that he did his morning routine without my help. My other duties as his wife were still met. I would take his breakfast, lunch, and dinner to him. Both of us were strong willed and equally stubborn. Therefore, we never spoke when I went to give him his food.

This morning though, I decided I should be the bigger person and go to him and express how disappointed I was with what he did. Just as I was about to get out of bed, my cell rang on the nightstand.

Picking up the device, my forehead creased with uncertainty looking at the name Sabrina and wondering who in the hell was this.

"Hello?" I answered after swiping the screen.

"Hey, Beautyful?" the female on the other end asked.

"Who's this again?"

"It's Sabrina, Toni's friend," she explained who she was, even though Toni would describe her differently. I slapped my hand against my forehead, feeling kind of dumb for not remembering her.

"Oh right, what's up, Sabrina?" I perked up, hoping she had some positive news for me.

"I think I found you somebody who can work with your husband."

Those words sent me flying in a seated position, forgetting about the insomnia I had been suffering from.

"Really? You did?" I whispered. It was like I was almost afraid that I heard her wrong.

"Yeah, her name is Keisha. I was telling her about your

husband's situation and she said she didn't mind helping y'all out. I can give you her number so you can holla at her right quick." Sabrina's words were like magic to my ears.

"Yes, that would be great. Thank you so much, Sabrina!" I gushed, forgetting immediately that my husband and I had beef. Hopping off the bed, almost falling in the process because the covers were wrapped around my ankles, I raced for a pen and a piece of paper and quickly jotted down the number Sabrina called out for me.

Thanking Sabrina again, I didn't waste any time to call the number that was just given.

"Hello, this is Keisha," the female voice at the other end answered after the third ring. I paused for a couple seconds because her voice sounded a little too sexy for me.

"Um, h-hi, hello. I got your number from Sabrina with regards to physical therapy for my husband," I said after my few seconds of hesitation.

"Oh yes! Hello, how are you? It's Beautyful...correct?" she asked in a cheerful voice.

"Um, right, yes it is."

"Your name is so unique. I love it. Please, tell me a little bit about your husband. Be specific about the type of injury he has and what progress he's made so far with his sessions."

Keisha and I were on the phone for an entire hour. I shared damn near everything with her and I could tell she listened to me attentively. She asked a lot of questions about Chaos and his condition, also about his attitude and how he has been feeling about losing mobility.

Keisha went on to explain that Chaos's anger was keeping him back and that was the first thing she needed him to address. I sighed softly because the three other therapists that tried to work with him failed in getting him to open up and accept that he no longer was the same person that could do everything on his own. He needed help if he wanted to get better. Keisha sounded like she knew what she was about and it was a plus that she had been a physical therapist for the past five years. Deciding to just bite the bullet, I went ahead and asked her if she could pop in and maybe see my husband so she would know what she was up against.

Agreeing to my request, Keisha told me she could make it over to our house within the next hour or so. Before we ended our call she gave me her price for her hourly session. Even though she was a bit pricier than the others before her, I didn't mind giving her a try.

That's when I got up and had a quick shower before taking my butt downstairs. I went to the kitchen to prepare his breakfast when an idea for a new pizza recipe hit me. I smiled because I couldn't wait to get started creating this recipe. Exactly one hour after my phone rang, it was Keisha saying she was out front.

Heading out of the kitchen, I made my way to the front door. Now, I am far from ugly. I might not have been built with a big ass and ridiculously thick thighs, but best believe I could shut shit down when I wasn't even trying to.

Even though I felt this way about myself and in no way was a self-conscious female, baby, when I opened that door and saw Keisha, I never felt like so much of an ugly duckling in all my life.

Chaos always boasted about me, claiming he had the baddest female in Philly, but when my eyes fell on Keisha, I began to second guess that title he gave me, which was fucking stupid.

She was drop-dead gorgeous with the most flawless skin I'd ever seen. Her facial routine must have included products from Milan, or she probably had baths in goat's milk or some shit. Her frontal wig flowed with soft curls down her back. She had a pair of bright, brown, soft eyes and her lips were shaped into a plump heart.

She was built like all she ate was cornbread and dumplings that went straight to her hips, thighs, and ass. Never had I ever felt insecure about my body, but here I was wishing my ass bigger and wishing my thighs were thicker.

"Beautyful?" she asked, smiling as she waited for me to introduce myself.

"Keisha, thank you so much for coming on such short notice. Please, come inside." I moved to let her get by.

I got a whiff of her Juicy Couture perfume as she glided by me. Her work scrubs showed off every curve she possessed on her body. Her big booty bounced up and down as she walked, letting me know her assets were probably real.

"Please, you can have a seat. I need a few minutes to go get my husband together. One thing I should say is that he has been a bit difficult in the past. Please do not let that get in the way of wanting to work with him." I wouldn't call what I said a warning, more like I was giving her a heads up.

"Trust me, I've seen it all before." She gave me a pitiful smile as though she knew and understood what I'd been dealing with.

Now that I've done my part and gotten yet another therapist to work with Chaos, I wondered if I was inviting trouble into my home. I really wasn't trying to be that wife. The petty wife that couldn't trust her husband around another pretty female.

I was trying not to be the wife that saw another gorgeous woman as a threat and competition. However, at the same time, what man wouldn't find Keisha attractive? Only a blind one maybe.

Sighing heavily, I threw the last of the wine down the back

of my throat. Pinching the bridge of my nose, I closed my eyes and wondered if I should stop drinking so much. Dealing with Chaos had me drinking a glass a day. Not to mention, I surprisingly started enjoying being in the kitchen. Something that was never my thing.

I smiled looking at the pizza dough. I really loved creating these different pizza flavors. Whenever I created a new one, I would take it to my sister and sometimes Toni to try. They would always tell me the same thing every time they were done devouring the triangular treat. They said I should really consider opening up my own pizza parlor.

Hearing them say that always gave me a boost of confidence because I was really thinking about doing just that. Matter of fact, I even began looking at spots on real estate sites that would be perfect for a pizza spot. Hopping off the counter, I placed my Tumbler in the sink and went to the fridge for my ingredients.

As I resumed rolling out the dough, I thought about what Chaos would say if I told him I wanted to start my business. I laughed to myself and shook my head, knowing that he would have an aneurysm before he gave at least one million reasons why it would be a bad idea. Truth was, I was getting tired of just being in the house all damn day.

At first, I can't even lie; I loved being taken care of. My man doing his thing while I went out with my sister and shopped and traveled from time to time with my girls. Going on expensive, lavish trips with my husband, all that was the shit. Then I started to miss having my own life, my own identity.

Sometimes I swear I walked in Chaos' shadow. I felt as though I gave up a lot for him as I watched him crave more money and more power. For instance, not only did I want to start having my own career but I also wanted us to start a family. One of the reasons I loved visiting my sister was so I could get to see my niece. Phoenix was such a vibe. I loved being around her and would spoil her as much as I could.

I've brought up trying to have a baby at least three times to Chaos but he always told me it wasn't the right time. That man was so focused on being the biggest drug dealer the U.S. has ever seen, at times my needs got pushed on the back burner.

I went to work spreading the tomato sauce, the cheese, at least three different types. Next I added onions, tomatoes, sweet peppers, and mushrooms. For the surprise, the meat was oxtail and small pieces of caramelized plantains.

I smiled as I admired my masterpiece that I named a taste of the Caribbean. The pizza oven that I got added recently to the kitchen was already preheated, so I popped my dough in and started cleaning up. Watching the time on my phone, I realized that Chaos's session had less than thirty minutes to go. I was super excited to see if he made any kind of progress.

Just as I began washing the dishes, my phone rang. Making my way over to where it was, I smiled when I saw it was my sister.

"Hey Lovely, what's up?" I asked, leaning against the granite counter.

"Is the therapist still there?" she questioned me, because of course I texted her and told her about Keisha.

"Yeah, they're still in the gym." I guess she must have sensed that I wasn't sounding as enthusiastic as I should.

"Why you sound like that?" she questioned me. I immediately began feeling stupid and hesitated to answer her question.

"Please, don't tell me DeAndre already showed his ass to that woman by acting a fool." I knew she was rolling her eyes just from her tone. I wouldn't say my sister hated my husband, but both she and our father thought I deserved way more than being the wife of a drug dealer.

"No, it's not that. It's kind of stupid really," I told her, covering my face, feeling embarrassed to confide in her about how I felt.

"Tell me what's up."

"I mean, she's really pretty. Like she reminds me of Carmelo Anthony's ex-wife, *what's her face*," I answered with a soft sigh, hating the fact that I was insecure about Keisha's presence.

The other therapists were one man and two women. However, the women looked nothing like Keisha. The first therapist was a middle-aged white woman with a lot of colorful tattoos littered all over her arms and neck. Matter of fact, Chaos mentioned that she gave off lesbian vibes. Obviously, I had no reason to worry there.

The second female was a pretty chocolate-colored girl. She was newly married and talked about her husband a lot. She definitely didn't give off any vibes that she was a cheater. I mean, she had just gotten married.

"You mean La La? Does she have the body to match or is she just pretty in the face?" my sister drilled me for answers.

"She has the entire package. I mean, she's here to do a job and I shouldn't be feeling like this, but I can't help it. Things between DeAndre and I haven't been the best either. I haven't said anything to you but I've been feeling lately that...I dunno —" I couldn't even finish my sentence as emotion clogged my throat, blocking the rest of my words.

"What have you been feeling lately? Talk to me, and when you're done, I'll share something with you." I giggled softly because my sister always did this, since we were kids. She would always try to get me to open up by promising me she would share some secret about her with me. It always worked.

"I dunno, I've been feeling as though DeAndre doesn't even love me anymore." Those words passing my lips seemed so surreal. I always felt like my husband and I would grow old together. Maybe even die hours apart like the couple from the movie *The Notebook*. Recently, it felt more like we could be headed for a divorce. "I wish he had never gotten shot. Shit went downhill from there."

I heard my sister sigh before she began talking. "Sis, I know I've given you shit for choosing DeAndre, but one thing I can say is that man loves you. His career choice can be better, but he loves you. I mean, if you are so worried about the therapist, ask her questions. Find out if she's married, if she's in a relationship, got kids, all of that. Get up in her business, just to be sure she's not on the market and looking to snatch herself a rich nigga. Then, we'll have to beat her ass just so she doesn't get any ideas about your husband." Lovely was going off and I raised an eyebrow at what she said.

Usually, I was the one that would be ready to act a fool, but hearing Lovely talk about beating people up raised a red flag.

"Ok, spill it. What's going on in your life that got you thinking you could swing on somebody?" I joked, walking over to the pizza oven to peep at how it was coming along. I smiled, loving the way it looked.

"I think Dorian is cheating on me," Lovely blurted out. I paused with my mouth hanging open from what she just admitted.

"Girl, what...are you sure?" I asked, stumbling toward one of the chairs at the island. I sat down with a loud plop.

"I mean, the signs are all there. All these extra training sessions, when he comes home he doesn't even come to bed. He sleeps in one of the guest bedrooms." She paused so she could take a deep breath.

Hearing her speak about her husband sleeping in a guest

bedroom made me think about my own situation with Chaos. Damn, we were living the exact same life.

"I keep seeing scratches on his back and shit. I mean, he comes back from practice and his hair is neat as fuck. Usually when he's back home after practice, he's normally a sweaty mess and I have to take his cornrows down and wash his hair. Lately, it's been different. I mean, am I tripping?" Lovely's voice cracked as though she was trying to hold back tears. I felt bad for my sister, knowing how much she loved her husband.

"Lovely, Dorian adores you and Phoenix. He's not like the other athletes that do stupid shit to jeopardize his marriage. I'm sure there's a reasonable explanation for what's been happening." I tried reassuring her as though my situation wasn't just as bad.

"I hope you're right sis, or else I'd have to kill him." She giggled a little, making me feel better that she wasn't too broken up about it.

"Ok, change of subject. I'm trying a new pizza recipe again," I gushed, walking back to the oven to stare at my masterpiece.

"I don't even care what it is. I want a slice." Lovely perked up even more. I smiled at her words because she loved sampling my new ideas.

"This time I decided to add small bits of caramelized plantains to my oxtail pizza," I bragged, checking the time, realizing that DeAndre's first session was about to be over.

"Oh shit, that sounds dope as fuck. I can't wait to try it."

"Sure thing. I gotta go sis, DeAndre's session is about to be over. The therapist hasn't run out screaming for bloody murder just yet, so I guess that's a good sign." I smiled, shaking my head at my ill-tempered husband.

"Let me know how it went. I love you and you know and I'm always a phone call away if ever you need a listening ear, alright." Lovely had been saying that to me ever since I confided to her how much DeAndre had changed after the shooting. She had no clue how much I appreciated her each time she uttered those words.

"I love you too, and the same goes for you. If ever you need to vent, just call me. I'm sure there's nothing to worry about with Dorian," I reassured her again before we said our goodbyes.

Knowing I needed to head over to the gym to see how things went with DeAndre's session, I waited five more minutes before heading over because I needed to take the pizza out the oven.

Once that was done, I took my apron off and began making my way toward the gym. For some odd reason I was super nervous as I got closer to the gym's door. Looking down at my attire, I then placed a nervous hand in my hair, wanting to look nothing but my best.

Rolling my eyes, I released a soft, nervous giggle because I suddenly felt silly about feeling insecure. Knocking on the door softly twice, I held the knob and slowly turned and it opened.

My first couple steps as I walked inside slowed down when I saw that Keisha was seated on the hardwood floor Indian style. DeAndre was in his wheelchair that was a couple feet away from her. DeAndre was looking down at her with a smile on his face as they chatted.

The way he was watching her with that smile on his lips made me scream in my head. Gone were the days when he looked at me like that.

When I say the pang of jealousy I felt at that sight made my chest constrict to the point where my fucking ribcage ached. It took Keisha a couple of seconds to even recognize I had walked in. Turning to me, her smile grew wider as she pushed her curvaceous body from off the floor.

"Hey, Mrs. Pereira. DeAndre and I are done for the day. We were just having a casual chat," she said with that stupid ass smile on her face. I wanted to knock that grin off her face.

My thoughts shocked me because this woman was here to do a job, no matter how I felt. From the looks of it, she'd had a successful first day because my husband was smiling again.

"Oh, that's wonderful." I tried my best not to let my true feelings show as I looked at my husband. DeAndre's smile slowly evaporated from off his face, and his expression returned to the same stoic one I've been seeing the past three months. "I'm happy that my husband seemed as though he's finally decided to behave." I smiled sweetly at him, hoping he would return the gesture. Unfortunately...he didn't.

"I would love to hear all about it as I walk you out," I offered Keisha, wanting her out of my house quickly before my jealousy ate me alive.

"Yes, sure. DeAndre, it was a pleasure working with you and I'll see you in the next three days," Keisha said, stretching her hand out so he could shake it.

I stood back and watched as DeAndre stuck his hand out and they shook each other's hands. Smiling, he told her he would see her soon.

"Do you need me to wheel you back to your bedroom?" I asked purposely so he could remove his hand from her own.

"Na, I'll stay here for a bit," DeAndre replied, placing his hands on his lap.

"Ok, let me walk you out so that I can pay you before you leave," I said to Keisha before I began walking out the room with her two steps behind.

"How was the session? Do you think he'll be back walking soon?" I desperately wanted to know the status of his health.

"Today was all about me and DeAndre connecting. So what I did was simply sit and talk to him so he could get comfortable with me. Once I get him to trust me, which I believe he did, at our next session I will begin the actual physical part of our therapy," Keisha explained, and once again, I felt a little uncomfortable.

Keisha and DeAndre just sat for an entire hour talking to each other. What the fuck! Were they on a fucking date? Then I had to pay her fifteen hundred dollars for that shit. Grabbing my purse as we entered the living room, I took out her payment.

"Thank you," Keisha said, taking the cash from me and heading to the front door. "By the way, DeAndre only had good things to say about you. He's lucky to have you by his side during his recovery. I have no doubt he'll be walking soon. Have a good day. See you on Friday." Keisha smiled sweetly at me before she walked off to where she parked her car.

Leaning on the back of the door, I folded my arms across my chest. I don't think I liked the fact that they were talking about me, even though she claimed DeAndre said only good things.

Deciding not to jump to any conclusions, I walked back to the gym to get DeAndre's side on how his therapy went. When I stepped into the room he was just sitting in his chair staring at his legs. My heart sank at the look on his face. I could only imagine how he felt at times losing his mobility.

"Hey," I called out to him softly. He hadn't even known I had walked into the room until I called out to him. Looking at me for a fleeting moment, I saw the man I fell in love with behind those eyes. Unfortunately, the softness of his brown eyes didn't last long, quickly replaced with a coldness.

"Hey," he answered, looking away from me as though my presence was a bother to him.

"How did you like your first session with Keisha?" I asked,

being sure my voice gave nothing away about feeling a type of way about her.

"It was aite, I guess. I just want to finally get out this fucking chair so I can find that mothafucka Pharaoh and lay him flat." DeAndre's voice was frigid, his thirst for revenge was impossible to believe.

Here I was wanting him out of that chair so we could continue living our life happily. Meanwhile, all this dumb ass had on his mind was revenge.

"I mean, don't you think you should use something else as motivation for you to walk again rather than seeking revenge, Chaos?" I walked over to his chair slowly with a small persuasive smile on my lips.

"What you think? That when I finally start walking again I'm just gone let that nigga go? You think I'm not about to do him the same shit he did to me and put his mothafucking ass in a wheelchair?" His face twisted with rage, and then he looked at me as though I was the stupidest bitch on the planet.

I sighed heavily with defeat while staring at him. "I don't even wanna fight with you, DeAndre. I just came to find out how you enjoyed your first session," I told him, defeated. Still trying to keep the peace, I slowly reached to place a hand on his shoulder.

"Well, if you don't want a fight, don't ever say no dumb shit like that. Pharaoh is a dead man as soon as I'm out of this chair," he sneered at me. My hand was just a couple inches from his shoulder, and I froze at his words.

I stared at DeAndre, feeling so confused and lost by his reaction to me. This man was just a few moments ago smiling and acting civilized with a complete stranger, a woman he only just met. Now, here he was with his nose turned up at me, his wife, the woman that loved him unconditionally who he was supposed to love back.

My heart literally broke at that moment and for the first time, I felt myself pulling away emotionally from my husband. Dropping my hand at my side, I took a deep breath.

"I'll see you later, DeAndre," I told him softly before I turned and walked out of the room.

CHAPTER NINE
TONI

I am strong, I am fierce, I am that bitch
I do not need a man to define me.

"I am strong..." I repeated the words of the recorded mantra I played every morning as I drove to work. I already dropped my son off at his daycare. Driving into the parking lot of my job, I quickly found a parking spot.

Cutting the engine off, I looked at my reflection in the rearview mirror, staring at my image. Sometimes it seemed as though I was the only one that could see the pain behind my eyes. The sad, trapped little girl that nobody knew was buried deep inside me.

Opening my Birkin bag, I fished out a lithium pill and popped one in my mouth, chasing it down with water from a bottle I kept in my car. I felt the capsule slowly make its way down my throat and plummet into my stomach. Once the pill was consumed, I prayed that today would be a good one. Lately, I felt myself slipping back into the darkness I fought so hard to pull myself out of. I couldn't let the darkness take me again...I've been doing so good.

Dropping the orange pill bottle back inside of one of the many overrated, expensive ass Birkin bag I owned, I hopped out my ride to begin my day. Plastering the smile on my lips that almost made me appear normal, the smile that people believed went all the way to my insides. I stepped confidently toward the front door. I clutched the handle of my briefcase in hand along with my handbag.

My expensive custom-made suit consisted of a knee-high skirt and shirt that hugged my 250-pound frame. Was I self-conscious because of my weight...fuck no! I was 5' 7" so my weight actually was evenly distributed throughout my body.

I had a pair of big bouncy titties, a not too flat stomach, curvy ass hips supporting a big juicy ass, and a pair of thick but firm, cellulite-free thighs. Can't anybody tell me shit to make me feel insecure about myself.

I was a bad mothafucking bitch!

I greeted everyone as I headed to the elevator, my fake smile going over their heads because they were either lost in their own worlds, or just didn't care enough to notice there was something I was hiding behind my tough exterior.

Standing inside of the elevator I shared with four other people, I kept my eyes on the display. Once the elevator dinged on the eighth floor, I walked out along with one other person onto the floor where I worked. From the moment my feet touched the lily white, shiny tiled floor I immediately realized something was wrong.

The air was different somehow, I felt it. My forehead creased as I saw everyone's attention in the conference room. My steps slowed down somewhat as I looked to where everybody was gawking at. The glass windows allowed me to see Mr. Owens, one of the senior lawyers, in a heated discussion with three members I recognized from the executive board.

My eyes narrowed with suspicion as I wondered what was

going on. Those three men from the board only made these appearances when somebody was in deep shit. Most times these kinds of meetings ended with somebody being fired.

Ignoring my other nosey coworkers, I walked past the conference room like nobody's business, because what was happening behind those walls had shit to do with me.

"Hey Latoya, hold my calls for the next fifteen minutes, ok," I spoke to my secretary as I walked up to her desk. She looked up at me and from her eyes, I could tell she wanted to fill me in on whatever the fuck had Mr. Owens in the meeting he was currently in.

Latoya knew better though, because she knew good and well I did not do office gossip. I told her if it had nothing to do with me then there's no reason I needed to know about it.

I raised my eyebrow at her when she failed to answer what I just requested.

"*Good morning*, and yes, I will hold your calls for the next fifteen minutes, Ms. Toni." She smiled at me even as she stressed on the good morning greeting. Stating the time of day was a greeting I seldom did, I just felt it was a waste of time. I mean, don't you know if it's morning, afternoon, or night time. Why do I have to tell you?

Huffing, not bothering to return her good morning, I stepped inside of my office. Waltzing over to my desk, I sat down in my gigantic, chocolate brown leather chair. Opening the bottom drawer, I placed my Birkin inside. I opened up my briefcase and took out my MacBook Air, flipping it upward, hitting the power button.

Grabbing my cup of coffee that must be there waiting for me placed by Latoya before I got to my desk, I grabbed the cup. Closing my eyes as the vanilla chai latte slipped past my lips and the warm brew entered my mouth.

Typing in my password, I waited for the laptop to start up.

My eyes shifted to the only thing on my desk, a framed photo. With no expression, I studied the three smiling faces behind the plastic that protected the photo.

This picture was the very last picture I'd taken. This picture was in happier times when my eyes didn't hide too much pain. Simply because I was genuinely happy here.

My fiancé sat in his mother's home on Christmas morning. She took the picture of me, Earon, and our son Aiden seated around the Christmas tree. We visited his mother every Christmas Day so she wouldn't have to be alone after her husband, Earon's father, died three years before of a stroke.

My eyes grew misty when I thought of how heartbroken she was when Earon died that night in his accident. She was so torn up over the death of her only child, her pride and joy, that she died six months after of a heart attack.

Earon's accident was something that I tried not to think about. That night lived rent free in my mind because I always felt like the accident was my fault.

Sniffing loudly, I blinked repeatedly, forcing away my tears because I did not have time for this. Sipping the last of my coffee, I turned my attention to my laptop ready to start my day. My last divorce case in which I won a nice settlement for my client was three days ago. I was supposed to start working on a new case this morning.

However, seeing that Mr. Owens, who was a senior partner and the person who was sort of my boss, was tied up, I had to wait until his meeting was over at the conference room so he could fill me in on what I'd be working on next.

Deciding to catch up on some of my emails, I opened my Gmail account. Not even five minutes in and the phone on my desk began ringing. Latoya was calling me and I was already annoyed because she knew not to disturb me when I asked specifically to be left alone.

"Didn't I—"

"They're asking everyone to come to the conference room for an emergency meeting," she cut off my chastising her by stating the purpose of her call before I asked.

"Great," I mumbled under my breath before putting the receiver down. I guess I was about to find out why Mr. Owens was in that meeting. Pushing my chair back, I disposed of the coffee cup in the waste paper bin under my desk. Walking to my door, I pulled it open and saw that Latoya was already gone.

Already annoyed by how my morning was going, I stepped toward the conference room door and walked inside of the already packed room.

I became even more irritated because all the seats were already gone and I had to stand. Doing a quick scan of the room, I realized Mr. Owens was no longer around, which could only mean one thing.

Just fucking great! I cursed in my head.

The three executives sat at the head of the table with very serious looks on all of their faces.

"We called this emergency meeting to inform you all that Jeffery Owens is no longer a partner at Fraser and Sons Ltd. After some thorough investigating, we found Mr. Owens practicing some unscrupulous acts that are not a positive representation of our firm, so we had to let him go," Mr. Jason Fitts addressed us, clearing the air so there would be no gossip.

"I will not go into further detail and instead would like to introduce the new senior partner that will be taking his place. The person a few of you will be working closely with." Mr. Fitts's eyes found me when he said that. Mainly because I worked under Mr. Owens. "Stanley, please bring Clarence in."

One of the other executives got up and briskly made his way out the door as everyone's eyes in the room followed.

Clarence, sounded like they went ahead and hired some fifty-something-year-old man that fussed about everything. Yay me!

The door reopened after a few seconds passed with Mr. Stanley walking in first followed by Clarence. I had to stop myself from allowing my eyes to pop out their sockets so my eyeballs wouldn't roll away on this tiled floor.

The room grew deathly still as this tall fine brother walked into the room. His confidence seeped through the expensive Gucci suit he wore. His right hand tucked inside of his pants pocket, and the pair of pants he wore fit his over six-feet-tall body to perfection.

A thick bush of well-maintained facial hair covered his handsome face, and his low fade was so fresh it looked as though he just got off the barber's chair. The more I looked at him the more I realized he kind of favored Morris Chestnut, and I loved me some Morris. Mr. Stanley offered him his seat and sat down, zero expression on his wonderful light-brown face.

He interlocked his fingers on top of the desk and I saw he had letters tattooed just under his knuckles, but I was too far to read what it said.

"Everyone, I would like to introduce Mr. Zayne Clarence. Our new senior partner."

Oh, his last name was Clarence, I thought as Mr. Fitts introduced him to everyone in the room.

"It's a pleasure to be here. I'm looking forward to working with some of you," Zayne addressed the room with his deep, somewhat husky voice. I could see the women swooning and I rolled my eyes at their silliness. I guess it was a bonus that he wore no ring on his finger, which indicated he wasn't married.

I tapped my feet softly as Mr. Fitts spoke for the next ten minutes. He spoke on a few changes that would take place effective immediately. I'm guessing this was based off whatever the fuck Mr. Owens did that caused him to end up in the unemployment office.

"Ok, thank you for your time on such short notice," Mr. Fitts said, indicating that the meeting was now over. I began to make my way out of the room, eager to get back to my desk. Standing in these heels for so long was murdering the soles of my feet.

"Um, Toni, a minute please."

Good lord almighty! I screamed in my head even as I smiled at Mr. Fitts, making my way over to them as everybody else left the conference room. I took a seat directly opposite Zayne. I felt his eyes on me as I kept my focus on the person who asked me to stay.

"Right, Toni, I wanted to personally introduce you to the person who you will be working with closely. Zayne, this Toni. Toni, say hello to Zayne." I turned my head slowly to the man that made me a little uncomfortable.

"Hello Zayne."

"Nice to meet you, Toni."

We both greeted each other almost simultaneously. On my lips was my usual smile, the smile that never reached my eyes. The smile that fooled everyone, but there was something about the way Zayne stared back at me. His gaze said he wasn't buying my award-winning smile. His eyes called bullshit on the mask I wore so proudly.

"Great, we'll leave you two to get better acquainted," Mr. Fitts said as the three men got up to leave. "Toni, Zayne will brief you on the new case you were supposed to be working on with Mr. Owens. Have a good day to you both." With those parting words they exited the room.

As I was now closer to Zayne, I could read the letters on his fingers. There was *love* tattooed on his right fingers and *life* tattooed on the left. Love life...I wondered what happened that made him get those thought-provoking words.

"Um, well, Mr. Owens usually emailed the info of my next client to me and I would start working on it immediately," I stated, wanting to get this ball rolling so I could get back to my office.

"Do I look like Mr. Owens?" His question was so blunt and abrupt that it threw me off a little. Actually, it threw me off a lot, because who was he speaking to like that?

"I wasn't implying that you were," I clarified, trying to hide the attitude in my voice. "I was simp—" Zayne held his hand up to stop me, and I quickly shut my mouth.

"First, let's get one thing straight. I'm nothing like the last senior partner that just got his ass fired over some foul shit." I tried to hide my shock at the way he spoke as though he was off the streets. "Second, how the last brotha did things, I can assure you, it's not how I'm about to do things," he said, leaning forward with an intense look in his eyes as the tip of his tongue flicked his bottom lip.

"O-ok." He managed to boil me down just like that.

"Perfect, now let me fill you in on your next client." Zayne took his cell phone out of his pocket as I sat back and waited for him to filter through his emails.

"Your client's name is Dorothy Chambers. She is divorcing Mr. Adam Chambers and requesting full spousal support, full custody of their kids, the house, the BMW, and the family dog Fufu. She will be here in the next two hours. I need you to tell me what strategies you plan on taking to ensure she walks away with what she's requesting. I expect you back in my office in the next half hour with your briefings on how you plan to win Ms. Dorothy everything she asked for," Zayne said in a dismissive tone as he began to stand up from behind the desk.

I made a snorting noise from deep in my throat because he had to be fucking kidding me. I usually took an entire day to come up with plans on how to go about winning my cases. This nut job wants my briefing in a half hour, he must be out of his fucking mind. The sound I made stopped Zayne from getting off his seat and he looked back at me.

"Is there a problem?" he asked me with his left eyebrow cocked in the air.

"As a matter of fact, there is. You cannot expect me to write up a plan for this case in thirty minutes. I mean, I haven't even met Ms. Dorothy. I have not spoken to her to get feedback on if what she's requesting from this divorce is even remotely possible," I replied, almost rolling my eyes at him because he was already riding my last nerve.

"Are you saying you can't do it?" he inquired.

"I'm saying...I need more time."

"Well, you don't have more time. The client will be here in the next two hours. When I got offered this position, I was told that you're the best junior lawyer in the firm. So far...I don't see it. I'll ask you again, are you saying you can't do it?" Zayne's voice was low and, to be honest, a little menacing. A staring match between us had me feeling as though I could strangle this man.

"No, I'm not saying that. I'll be back with my notes in the next half hour." *You fucking asshole!* I screamed in my head, wishing I could say that to him.

"Great, I'm looking forward to reading your notes. Now, if you'll excuse me, I have other workers I need to meet," Zayne's obnoxious ass said before getting up from his chair.

I sat back as I watched him make his exit and exhaled slowly through my mouth. I was supposed to work with that cocky nigga? I do believe I would rather dig my own eyeballs out.

Zayne sure was a piece of work. I could tell by his assertiveness he was probably one of those men that called themselves Alpha males. I smiled to myself as I got up from my desk, preparing to make my way back to my office.

Zayne and I were about to lock horns if he kept up with his controlling ways bullshit. I wasn't worried though because I was ready to show him he never met a female like me.

CHAPTER TEN
CHAOS

Today was going to be the second therapy session with Keisha. I turned to the empty spot on my bed where Beautyful should be but she wasn't.

My right hand supported the back of my head as I stared at the roof of the guest bedroom. Looking at nothing in particular, I slowly realized that my wife and I were having problems. Since three days ago, after my therapy session, Beautyful had been avoiding me.

The routine things she did like feed me were still happening, but other than being fed she turned into a mute. If my wife wasn't upstairs in the room doing God knows what, I sometimes found her in the kitchen dabbling with a new pizza recipe. I sighed heavily because I knew I was the one responsible for her change.

As much as I was trying not to take my frustrations out on my wife, it was hard because I was so angry all the time. Then when Beautyful suggested that I forget about seeking revenge on Pharaoh, I fucking lost it. How could she even propose something so fucking ridiculous?

My wife knew the type of nigga she married. I was a mothafucking gangsta! I sold my illegal drugs and became a millionaire off that shit. What type of punk did Beautyful take me for? Like I was really about to give the nigga that almost left me paralyzed a hall pass!

Fuck no! So if she didn't get that then maybe she didn't get me. If that was the case, maybe we really shouldn't even keep entertaining this marriage. The thought of Beautyful not being my wife anymore made me panic a little. I literally felt the anxiety rising in my throat. I pushed the thought to the back of my mind, deciding not to think too irrationally.

Pushing that thought back brought another one forward. That thought had a pretty face and a banging body. Finding out that Beautyful once again got me another therapist had me seeing stars. However, when I saw what my new therapist looked like...a strange feeling came over me.

Men like me always had a bad reputation; drug dealers were never faithful. Where the fuck was that ever heard? It's not like I never fucked a couple different women a few days or maybe even a few hours apart. However, when a bitch is just a jump off, I let that be known off the bat. I don't like confused women in my face asking me why I didn't pick up my phone when they were calling me last night. I would definitely hurt a bitch's feelings and let them know it was because I was knee deep in some other female's tight box.

Beautyful, on the other hand, she weaved her magic spell on a nigga. I was sprung off her so bad that when I got the opportunity to lock her fine ass down...that's what the fuck I did. I could brag on any given day that I'd never cheated on my wife. I loved, respected, and appreciated her so much. I didn't want to lose her. I wanted the kind of love my parents had, that everlasting type shit.

So when I got the strangest feeling in the pit of my stomach after I laid eyes on Keisha, that shit confused me. It didn't help either when Keisha said she hadn't planned on actually beginning the physical part of my session that day. She explained firstly that she was going to do mental and emotional therapy.

I looked at her as though she had lost her mind. Because what the fuck was mental and emotional therapy? Then she looked me dead in my eyes and said, *tell me really how mad are you that you can't walk again.*

That simple question made up of twelve words had never been asked of me before. I've been asked everything except that, and finally this complete stranger asked me.

It felt refreshing, it was like someone finally fucking understood me and what I was going through. Everyone I knew just kept telling me the same shit, you need to focus more so you'll walk again. If I had a million dollars for every time Beautyful told me my paralysis was only temporary and I wasn't trying hard enough, I'd be a billionaire.

Every time she told me that shit, my blood boiled. She had no idea the many times I laid in this very bed with her next to me as I tried to wiggle my toes. She didn't know how badly I wanted to reach for her, strip her naked, climb on top, and fuck the shit out of her until she begged me to stop.

So to hear her say that I wasn't trying hard enough made me despise her for saying so. Keisha's question made me *word vomit*, and I released the pent-up frustration of not being able to walk on her. She never interrupted me, she never told me I wasn't trying hard enough because my symptoms were temporary. All Keisha did was listen to me.

Twenty minutes later when I was done, she smiled at me and said, *cool, do you know of any good tattoo shops? I need some new ink work done.*

On God, I felt as though Keisha was dope as fuck. She was easy to talk to. So we sat there and chopped it up until my hour was up, talking mostly about tattoos, piercings, and what dope eating spots we liked best in Philly.

I did learn she had a nigga and no kids, but she seemed not to want to talk about him too much, not that I wanted her to anyway. Talking to Keisha was the most relaxed I'd been in a minute. Low-key, I was excited as fuck to have this second session with her.

Deciding it was time to get up from the bed to take care of my hygiene, I threw the covers off me. Hooking my hands around my knees, I was about to drag my legs off the bed when something strange happened.

I hit the toes of my right foot on the bedframe, and it hurt.

"Ow, fuck," I muttered, but then I paused. It took a couple seconds, but then it hit me that I felt that!

Squinting my eyes, I focused on my toes really hard and willed myself to wiggle them.

I gasped loudly when they actually moved. Just to be sure I wasn't imagining the shit, I did it again. Like the first time my toes moved a second time.

"Get the fuck outta here," I mumbled to myself, cheesing hard as hell at the sight of my toes with actual movement. I was so amped I wanted to shout out to Beautyful for her to see what I could do.

Unfortunately, she wasn't doing too much talking where I was concerned, so I decided to share my news with her later. Dragging my legs off the bed, I reached for the wheelchair and pulled it as close to me as I could.

With a determined mind, I managed to get myself onto the wheelchair without falling on my face.

Beautyful never came to assist me this time. I still achieved everything I had to do on my own. I was as stubborn as they come and wasn't about to holla at my wife for her help. Wheeling myself toward the kitchen, I found a note on the small dining table in the middle of the kitchen. With a deep crease in my forehead, I picked it up and read it.

Your breakfast is in the microwave. I'll be down when it's time for Keisha to get here. I'm handling some stuff.

Not sure how to feel about her note, I tossed it back on the tabletop. Wheeling myself to the microwave, I opened the door to see a plate with scrambled eggs, bacon, and two pieces of toast. Even though I was hungry as hell, I turned my nose up at the food.

The fuck is going on with my wife. She knew I hated bacon. I had no clue why she put two strips of the shit on that plate. Sucking my teeth, I slammed the microwave door and wheeled over to a bowl of fruit on the other side of the kitchen. Grabbing an apple, I went into the living room. As I took a bite of my fruit, I watched the stairlift. The chair was at the bottom of the stairs waiting to be sat in.

Slowly, my eyes traveled up the stairs and I wondered what the fuck was she even doing up there? What had her so busy that she couldn't come down to help me get ready for my therapy session?

Squinting my eyes up the stairs that led to the hallway, my mind began to stray. Eating the last of my apple, I dropped the core on my lap and took a rolled-up blunt from behind my ear.

What if she had another nigga up there? I took a lighter from my sweatpants pocket and lit my blunt. Inhaling deeply, I looked at the chair on the lift and contemplated sitting on there and going up to see what the fuck my wife was doing.

Matter of fact, I was going to remain in this very spot so if she did have a nigga up there, I would see who the fuck it was. A few seconds later I cursed myself in my head because I knew my wife wouldn't do any crazy shit like that. Being in this wheelchair was beginning to make me go a little *cuckoo*.

Besides, Beautyful knew I'd kill her and her side nigga...if she ever thought about having one.

Finishing off the last of my blunt, I remained in the living room with the TV on, but I wasn't paying attention to what was playing. I was more focused on wiggling my toes every half hour to make sure I still had movement in them. The doctor that attended to me when I got shot told me that I would get some spastic movement over time, where my legs or toes may just spasm uncontrollably, but I don't think this was that.

I became lost in my own world and what would be the first thing I planned on doing once I could walk again. Rubbing my facial hair while I pondered, I realized I needed to get myself in order.

Fishing my phone from out my sweatpants pocket, I dialed Bjorn's number.

"Sup, my nigga," he answered on the second ring.

"Ayo, I'mma need for you to get Carlos to come over and line me up right quick," I told him, raking my fingers through my matted beard. I really was tweaking letting this shit grow out like wild bush.

"Say word! You sound different, like your old self again. What brought about this change?" Bjorn asked, bringing a smile to my face as I looked down at my feet.

"I'm just tired of looking in the mirror and getting scared at the werewolf looking back at me," I cracked, deciding that I'd hold up on sharing the news of regaining feeling and movement in my toes. I would wait for Keisha and hear what her thoughts were.

"I feel you. I'll call Carlos now and set it up. I'll text you back the time he'll be over at your house."

"Hol'up. What about that nigga? Any word on where the

fuck he's at?" My mood shifted that quickly when I mentioned Pharaoh. A dark feeling instantly took over me.

"I'm working on something. I should get some news maybe in a week's time. I haven't forgotten. That nigga's not about to get away with what he did to you and Animal." Bjorn's words didn't make me feel any better. I needed that nigga's head on a platter.

"Aite, bet. One other thing, I'm calling up the connect today to work on a shipment. We're about to be back, my nigga," I informed him as I nodded my head. Footsteps descending the stairs drew my attention and I turned my head, knowing it was my wife.

"I gotta go, but we'll talk more on this later." Before Bjorn could respond, I ended the call just as Beautyful's feet hit the last step. Using my thumb and index fingers, I pinched my lower lip as I studied her, tilting my head to one side.

"Going somewhere?" I asked, trying to hide my anger. Looking at me with a few feet between us, she stood in a pinstriped skirt suit that fit her like a glove. The skirt stopped just above her knees, the jacket hugged her upper body. With only two buttons it opened enough to show off her firm, ample breasts. Her curly hair framed her face and her bangs stopped just on her eyebrows.

With a Hermes handbag draped in the crook of her arm, she looked like a million dollars. If I didn't know any better, I'd think she was going to work or some sort of business meeting.

"As a matter of fact, I am. Keisha just called and said she'll be here soon. I'll take you both to the gym and then I'll be gone for about forty-five minutes. I'll be back before Keisha leaves." Her reply felt as if she was trying to be vague on purpose, which only irritated me further.

"That still doesn't answer my question of where you're going." On God, I almost thought of standing up from this chair to grab her by her shoulders. The reality of my situation quickly popped that fucking bubble.

"I'm accompanying Lovely on some sort of new business venture she's thinking about. That's all, Chaos," she replied just as a knock sounded at the door. Before giving me a chance to question her some more, she walked toward the front door.

My teeth sunk even deeper into my lower lip because I knew my wife and I knew she was lying. I knew damn well Beautyful didn't have the guts to strike up some sort of relationship with another nigga while I was stuck in this chair.

Na, my wife wouldn't be so mothafucking crazy. She was hiding something from me though, and all that did was give me more ammunition to speed up the process of me walking again.

"And how is my favorite patient this afternoon?" Keisha waltzed into the living room, her scrubs hugging her figure, a bright smile on her face. Beautyful tagged behind her, eyeing me in a suspicious manner.

"I'm straight," I replied, my eyes moving from my wife to Keisha's as she came up to my chair. The fragrance of her perfume reminded me of warm vanilla and brown sugar. I wiggled slightly in my chair, suddenly feeling uncomfortable.

"Let me walk you both over to the gym," Beautyful said, leading the way, not waiting for either of us to reply. *She sure seemed in a hurry*, I thought as Keisha took hold of the handles of my chair and trailed behind my wife.

"I hope you have a good session, DeAndre," Beautyful said, standing back as she opened the door to the gym so Keisha and I could get by.

"Don't worry, his session will be a little more intense than my last visit," Keisha reassured her as she began setting up. My eyes fell on my wife and she looked my way. Slowly, she made her way over to me and bent, placing a soft kiss on my lips.

Before she could move away from me, I held onto her chin firmly and looked deeply into her eyes.

"I want you to remember that you're still my wife." My words were direct and dripped with malice. Just in case she started to get any ideas on being unfaithful. I saw the moment when fear entered her eyes even for just one second before I released her chin.

Straightening up, she lifted her head in a haughty manner before she turned to Keisha. "I'll be back soon," were her last words before she hastily left the room.

Exhaling softly, I kept my composure as Keisha made her way toward me. There was an examination-type table Beautyful placed in the gym, and Keisha began to take me over there.

"I wiggled my toes earlier," I told her, and she paused with her mouth slightly open.

"Are you serious?" she gasped in shock, looking down at my feet that were covered with a pair of lily-white socks. I nodded my head at her and she bent to remove the cotton barrier off my feet.

"Can you do it for me?" We both had our eyes on my feet and slowly I moved my toes back and forth.

"This is huge. I have a massage planned for you. It's even going to be a lot more successful now that you're regaining feelings and movement to certain parts of your feet." Keisha was smiling even harder than I was this morning.

Taking my chair over to table, she stood up with a serious look on her face.

"Ok, so I have to get you off the chair and onto the table. Don't worry, I've done stuff like this thousands of times. I'll just need you to help me as much as you can." I nodded my head in agreement, already hating that she had to physically lift me out.

"One...two...three." She did a silly countdown with her hands tucked under my arms. Pushing myself up, I helped her the best that I could and some way or another, she actually got me seated onto the table. Then she lifted my feet and placed them flat so I had to lie back. She made it seem way easier than I would have imagined.

"See, I told you I've done this many times before," she said, winking at me while she giggled. "Ok, now relax. I have to remove your sweatpants."

Those words made me tense up a bit because I thought she was probably only going to massage my feet or some shit. She probably sensed my apprehension and smiled.

"Massages assist with proper circulation," she explained with her hands already at the waistband of my pants. She began tugging them down as I laid looking up at the roof of the gym. "I'm just going to turn you from one side to the next so I can roll your pants all the way down."

The touch of her fingers against the coolness of my bare skin made me get goosebumps. I thanked God I chose a pair of Gucci boxers to wear today and not my fruit of the looms which I normally wore at home.

"Ok, let me get my oil and we'll start." I've never felt this naked while still being clothed in my entire life. I was as still as a leaf when Keisha bent a little next to me with a bottle of massage oil in her hands.

I listened as she flipped the cap and squeezed some of the liquid into the palm of her hands. For some strange reason, the sound was intensified times 100.

"Ok, I'll start at your feet and work my way up, alright." I nodded my head as I swallowed a lump in my throat. The warm touch of her hands rubbing my left foot made me close my eyes briefly.

"Do you feel me touching you?" she asked softly, her question sounding far too erotic. Or was it just me that thought so? I mean, she was just doing her job.

"Yeah, I do."

"That's really awesome that you can feel me," she replied, and once again it sounded sexual as fuck. I managed to control my breathing as her fingers did their magic. She ran her fingers between my toes, the sole of my foot, and then my heel. Then she slowly rotated it over and over before her hands slowly traveled up to my calf.

By the time she was ready to massage above my knee, I was so relaxed that I almost drifted off to sleep. Until I felt her shove my boxers up, exposing my upper thigh some more.

Fuck, what if I fucked around and got an erection? I thought to myself, terrified. *What the fuck was a nigga even to say or do if some shit like that happened?*

The wheels on the bus go round and round...

I don't even know why that stupid ass song of all songs popped in my head when her hands began to rub into my flesh.

"Can you feel my touch here?" she asked me again. I shook my head no because the only reason I knew she was rubbing my upper thigh was because I was looking at her.

"That's ok, I have faith your feeling will be back sooner rather than later," she reassured me with a smile. My dick remained on its best behavior for my left leg massage. Now, she was about to do the right side.

Once again, she began with my foot. Applying pressure with her fingertips as she asked again if I could feel her touch. I answered once more that I could.

"Ok great. That's good," she whispered.

She suddenly seemed to have lost her balance and she fell forward a little. Unfortunately for me, when that occurred, her breasts brushed lightly against my toes, rubbing up against them.

Oh, fuck my life! I screamed in my head when I felt my body tense up and before I knew what was happening, my body began to react.

Instead of looking at her hands at work, my goofy ass kept looking at her breasts. By the time she made her way to my upper thigh and she began to shove my boxers up, she saw that I had an erection. Even with my hands trying to hide it.

"I-I-I'm sorry. It just sort of happened," I stammered, trying not to look at her. I was sure I was about to be the first nigga to die of fucking embarrassment. My death certificate was legit about to say, *cause of death…embarrassment*.

"As I said, I've done this a million times already. Stuff like this is normal and very healthy. It's good to see that…other things still work," she smiled, blushing a little. "Um, I have to go to the bathroom anyway. That should be enough time to get you situated. When I come back, we'll move on to some leg stretches, ok."

Closing the massage oil, she placed it next to me. I watched in silence as she exited the room so she could go use the guest bathroom downstairs.

Exhaling loudly, I looked down at my dick and raised the waistband of my boxers.

"Nice going, your timing is off as fuck," I chastised my manhood while I thought of the time I walked in on my grandmother changing when I was ten years old. That did the trick, my dick got soft in no time.

CHAPTER ELEVEN
BEAUTYFUL

"Oh shit," I moaned when Chaos inserted the vibrating dildo inside of me. I began backing away from the intensity of the device because I swore I would pass the fuck out.

"The fuck you going?" he asked, grabbing my upper thigh and squeezing into my flesh. Forcing me to stop backing away from him and the sinful act he was committing on me.

Clawing at the cushions on his sofa, my hips began to move in a rhythm with the dildo. I have never used such a thing in my life. Normally, I would use my fingers to masturbate and that was it. This right here that this man was doing to me was a new experience. One that I was enjoying tremendously.

"You like that?" he asked me, pausing the device as it vibrated my insides. I nodded my head vigorously, answering his question the best that I could.

"Na, use your words for me," he instructed me before using the tip of his tongue to flick my clit.

"Aaaahhh," I cried out as a burst of colors flashed before my eyes. I immediately closed my eyes because I just knew I was about to die. This man's sexual expertise was about to take me to meet my maker.

"Don't close your eyes. Look at me," he commanded, and I did as I was told.

Gazing down at him as he held the vibrator in me had to be the most erotic thing I've ever experienced in my life.

"You're about to be my wife."

He licked my clit with the tip of his tongue as he slowly pumped the vibrator in and out.

"You're about to be mine and only mine."

He plucked my clit between his lips, repeatedly playing with it. I released a silent scream, not a single sound passed my lips.

"Nothing and nobody is going to stop me from claiming you as my own, Beautyful."

My orgasm hit then. Hard, rocking my body as I writhed against his mouth. Panting and begging, sometimes speaking words that made no sense.

I had no idea when he even removed the dildo and replaced it with his own dick. I was too far gone. It was indeed shameful. My knees were to my chest as Chaos fucked the living daylights out of me.

My wrists were pinned above my head while he grunted in my ear. His dick was big, bigger than any other I've experienced. It stretched me out to the point where it hurt...but I didn't care.

"I could tell this pussy has never been fucked right," Chaos whispered naughtily in my ear as he thrusted even deeper in me.

"Every time you move for the next three days, I want you to remember that I was here," he said, slowing down his movements before picking back up the pace.

Wrapping his hand around my throat, his other hand still had my wrists pinned above my head, I felt him swell inside of me and then he began sucking my neck.

"Fffffffuckkkk," he grunted as he came inside me.

"Mmmmm," I moaned, lifting my hips against my fingers as I orgasmed. The memory of the first time Chaos and I fucked replayed in my head as I masturbated in my bed.

Panting slowly, I removed my fingers from out my underwear and opened my eyes. At that very moment, silent tears rolled down my cheeks and I wasn't even sure why I was crying.

It could have been so many different reasons but no matter what reason it was, the source of my tears, the root of it all, was one person, DeAndre Pereira.

Today was supposed to be a good day. Wiping my tears away, I got up ready to face the day with a newfound determination. I planned to stay away once again and allow Chaos to see about himself. It was still early so I went downstairs to the kitchen and made him breakfast.

Just to be extra petty, I added two strips of bacon to his eggs, knowing damn well he hated bacon. As I made my way back up the stairs, I was tempted to check in on him but I changed my mind.

I took my sweet time getting dressed. While I was buttoning my jacket my cell began ringing. Answering Keisha's call, she let me know she was a few minutes away.

Satisfied with the reflection looking back at me from the floor-length mirror, I picked up my Hermes handbag, one of many gifted to me by Chaos, and made my way down the stairs.

My husband was all dressed and waiting for his session with Keisha to begin. Immediately I could feel his eyes on me, but this morning I refused to get into it with him. When he questioned me about my whereabouts, I had no choice but to lie and not be completely honest. I knew Chaos all too well and I knew he didn't believe shit I said. He probably thought I had started seeing someone else.

I did my wifely duties and even kissed Chaos before I left. Him grabbing my chin with the warning look and his intimidating words, *"I want you to remember that you're still my wife,"* was a subtle warning that told me he thought I was cheating on him. He couldn't be more wrong, but I wasn't about to clarify shit.

As I drove to meet a real estate agent, both my mind and heart were heavy. I felt as though I was drowning in a whirlwind of emotions, losing my grip on reality.

Exhaling slowly, I turned the volume up on my radio and sang along with my girl Mary J. Blige.

"How can I love somebody else, if I can't love myself enough to know when it's time, time to let go. Sing, all I really want is to be happy..."

Twenty minutes later I was standing in an empty building with a wide smile on my face.

"I love it. What do you think?" I turned to my sister as she scanned the spot that I wanted to lease for my pizza shop I decided I was opening.

"I think it's just the right size for a first-time restaurant owner. I say go for it," Lovely gave her approval, cheesing at me. The realtor stood a couple feet away waiting for my decision.

"Have you spoken to him yet?" Lovely asked me, and I immediately looked away from her. "Aw, come on, Beautyful. What the fuck are you waiting on? The longer you wait the harder it's gonna be to let Chaos know you plan on starting up your own business."

"Don't you think I know that?" I huffed at her, folding my arms under my breasts. It was bad enough I had to lie to him just now. Keeping something like this from him was not going to end well for me, I already knew that.

"Do you need more time, Mrs. Pereira?" the agent named

Sherry Smith asked me. "I can maybe block this spot for you for say three days, a week tops, but no longer than that. The location is a prime spot and businesses on this strip strive within the first three months of opening," she explained, stepping closer to me.

Sighing softly, I looked around the room and I could just picture how great it would look once I finished furnishing the place. I really wanted this. My pizza recipes had been blowing up after I created an Instagram page to share pictures of my original creations. I managed to steer clear away from social media until now.

When I started the page named A Beautyful Slice of Heaven, I had no clue I would have gotten the response I did. I had people asking me where my shop was located, if I did catering for birthday parties and functions, what were my prices. It was overwhelming, so I decided to take a risk, a huge leap of faith, and search for a place where I could open up my very own pizza parlor.

"Yes, please just give me three days maximum, and I'll have a final answer for you," I pleaded with my hands clasped together, looking at Sherry with pitiful eyes.

"Ok, but no longer than that."

"Thank you so much. I really do appreciate it," I gushed, shaking her hand a little too rigorously. "Shit, I'm sorry," I apologized once I realized I almost shook her hand right out of its socket.

The three of us walked out of the building. Sherry and I said our goodbyes before she hopped in her Honda and drove off. My sister and I stood next to my car as I admired the property I hoped would be mine one day.

"I've never seen you this excited about something, sis." Lovely reached over and squeezed my shoulder.

"I really want this, Lovely. After I got married to Chaos, I dunno, it's like I lost myself somehow. Everything was always about him. I tried to be the type of wife he wanted but not the wife *I* wanted to be. Some may call me ungrateful because I don't appreciate being a kept woman. But I never wanted to be a trophy wife as people will call it. I just wanted to go on being me and somewhere along the way...I lost that," I explained, staring at the building I knew would be my future soon.

"Trust me, I get it. We both practically are living the same life." I turned to my sister and she had somewhat of a sad expression on her face.

"We'll figure this all out one day, sis." I reached over and hugged my big sister close to me. "At least you have Phoenix. I don't even have a dog or even a goldfish," I said, pouting my bottom lip out, feeling sorry for myself.

"Damn, when was the last time you even had sex? You'd have to be fucking in order to bring life into the world. You remember at least that much, right? That you needed to have sex in order to bring life into the world," Lovely was making fun of something I didn't find funny in the least.

"I swear to God, I'm horny all the fucking time. My rose vibrator is about to wither and die soon." I covered my face, but not from embarrassment, because my sister and I shared everything with each other. It was more out of frustration for all the things I'd been dealing with lately.

"Maybe that's it. That's what you need to do." Lovely grabbed my upper arms, forcing me to face her. A surprised look emerged on my face as I stared into her excited eyes, not sure what the fuck was happening.

"What are you talking about?" I questioned her.

"Give that man some pussy. Throw that good cat on him. I mean, I'm sure he's horny just like you. When you get home, put it on him like you know he'd like it. You have needs too. Just because his goofy ass is feeling some type of way about his paralysis doesn't mean he should keep depriving you like this. Then, when you give him that good bedroom workout...whala!" she said with her arms outstretched at the building we were standing in front of.

"Tell him about this and what you plan on doing with it. You know the saying, *'sometimes you have to use what you have to get what you want.'*" She winked at me before giggling at what she thought I should do.

"You think that will work?" I asked her, thinking long and hard about what she said. I turned to face my sister slowly, gnawing at my lower lip thoughtfully.

"There's only one way to find out. Let's go," she grabbed my hand and we briskly made our way to our parked vehicles.

"Are you insane?" I snatched the scrap of material from out of Lovely's hand. My eyes damn near bulging out their sockets.

"Girl, you trying for that man to say yes to you starting a career again or no?" She grabbed the lingerie back from out of my hands and held it up in the air as if I wasn't embarrassed enough.

After we left the viewing of the building my sister insisted we make our way to the mall. She said I needed to give Chaos added inspiration to say yes when I asked him. Her idea of inspiration was the most ridiculous lingerie I'd ever seen in my life.

"Where does my body parts even go?" I asked, tilting my head from one side to the next in the lingerie store as I inspected the lace getup.

"It's a whole bodysuit type thing, Beautyful. Your tits go here, your pussy will be right here," Lovely pointed out where certain body parts were supposed to go. I squinted and then blushed because it was obvious my breasts would be completely out and so would my vagina because this outfit had no crotch. As a matter of fact it had no anything, just a bunch of straps zig zagging about. "Easy access for DeAndre. There's no need for him to remove anything to get to the good parts."

I laughed with a shake of my head as I took the lingerie out of her hands.

"There's one more thing I think you should get," Lovely suggested before disappearing. Sighing softly, I studied the clothing in my hand, knowing it would probably take me an hour to figure out how to even get into this shit.

A white box was suddenly thrust in my face with a picture of a bright pink dildo glaring at me.

"Jesus," I giggled, snatching the box out of my sister's hand as I inspected the vibrating dildo. I couldn't even front, Chaos would love this. Whether it was me using it on myself with him watching or him using it on me, he loved freaky shit like that.

"You're the one that told me your man welcomed sex toys. Go nuts tonight. Now, let's go cash out. I'm buying you the dildo, by the way. Just call it the gift that keeps on giving," she giggled when she saw the look on my face as we began making our way toward the cashier.

"When did you get like this?" We both fell out laughing, approaching the young cashier who looked at us in curiosity.

I paced the floor of my bedroom, feeling really stupid that I was actually about to do this. For the hundredth time, I paused in front of the full-length mirror and stared at my reflection.

This lingerie with matching robe set a bitch back $500. I

looked at the new vibrator rabbit Lovely bought me laid out in the middle of the bed like some prized possession.

Lovely had kept me so long at the mall that by the time I got back Keisha had already gone, leaving DeAndre with the task of paying her.

Thinking about DeAndre made a frown form on my face because since I got home he had been acting pretty strange. I tried asking him about his session and what was done, but he brushed me off, refusing to answer me. He even seemed a little uncomfortable somehow when I asked him about Keisha and how she said he was progressing.

I even tried calling Keisha twice to ask her if there was any improvement with his paralysis, but her phone went straight to voicemail. Hopefully, what I was about to do to him would warm him up enough to make him want to open up to me.

Why was I so nervous? I was acting as though this wasn't my husband that I hadn't been married to for the past three years. My four-inch heels clicked loudly as I walked to the bed and picked up the vibrator.

Shoving the sex toy inside the pocket of my robe, I walked toward the stairs. I took my sweet time descending the steps just so I wouldn't tumble my clumsy ass the rest of the way down.

I headed toward DeAndre's room then made a beeline to the kitchen so I could take a drink of wine to calm my nerves. I could always count on my Tumbler bottle to have alcohol instead of water inside. I drank the entire thing, closing my eyes, enjoying the warmth running through me. With a newfound confidence, I stepped toward Chaos' door and knocked on it lightly.

God, what if he was asleep already? What do I do then? I hadn't even considered that.

"Yeah," his raspy voice called out. Closing my eyes, I

exhaled slowly from my mouth, turned the knob, and stepped inside. The smell of weed hit my nose immediately.

The way my mouth went dry at the sight of him. He was in a seated position on the bed as he smoked his blunt. He was naked from the waist up, showing off his toned upper body. His tattoo sleeve and neck ink work glistened under the warm light of the room.

When he saw me I could tell he was taken aback because his hand paused just as he was about to put the joint to his lips.

The wine had begun to take effect and the shyness I felt a few moments ago dissipated. Slowly, I walked over to the bed. His boxers clung to his toned thighs, outlining the dick I was yearning for like a crackhead.

He squinted his eyes before dipping his head back a little to blow smoke into the air.

"What's all this?" he asked, licking his lips. His eyes lazily ran over my barely dressed body. With confidence I didn't even know I had, I got closer to him so that I could take the blunt from out his fingers.

Never taking my eyes off his, I placed it to my lips and inhaled deeply before blowing the smoke in my husband's face. Handing the blunt back to him, I licked my lips seductively.

"I came to show you something," I told him with my fingers on the tie that held my robe in place.

"Oh yeah. What's that?" Chaos asked with a tilt of his head.

Taking the robe off, I allowed it to fall to the floor around my ankles. The sex toy was securely in my hand. His pupils dilated when he saw the scrap of clothing I was wearing. With my titties exposed and pussy out on display, I knew he wouldn't be able to resist by the way he was staring at my body.

"I came to show you what you've been missing." I made sure to lock eyes with him as I held the vibrator up to my mouth. Using my tongue, I licked it hungrily. I could tell I was beginning to affect him by the way his breathing pattern changed.

Climbing onto the bed, I sat spread eagled between his feet, giving him an excellent view of the show, I was about to put on for him. Licking his full lips, he eyed my moist pussy greedily.

Bringing the vibrator to life with a push of the power button, DeAndre smoked his blunt as I used the tip of the toy to run against my nipples. My lips parted slightly, the rush of the vibrating sensation woke my body up, making my nipples harden instantly.

Running the toy between my breasts making following the path from my stomach to my pulsing lower region, I wasted no time burying the vibrating device deep inside the tightness that hadn't been touched by my husband in a while.

"Mmmm," I moaned lustfully as the toy buzzed inside of me, making me thrust my hips forward. With the other tip I placed it on my clit and I almost came instantly.

"Oh shit," I gasped, closing my eyes as I dipped my head back.

"Na, open those pretty fucking eyes and look at me," Chaos demanded, and I immediately did as I was told. His eyes were hooded with desire, his hand now resting on his obvious erection. He was no longer smoking.

Gasping loudly while I held the vibrator in place, Chaos and I held each other's eyes. My hips moved in a circular motion as I brought myself closer to the edge. With my free hand I played with my breasts, plucking my nipples until they hurt.

"I wanna cum with you inside of me," I pleaded with him, needing to feel him because I missed him so much.

"Come here," he called me over. Beckoning me with his index finger before pulling his dick out of his boxers. Turning the toy off I tossed it aside, hurriedly I crawled over to him, straddling his body. Positioning myself over him as I held his thick, meaty dick in my hand. Licking my lips as the tips of my fingers brushed the huge bulging veins on his shaft.

With our eyes locked in with each other's, I released a contented sigh as his nine inches entered me. The tightness of my walls protesting at first after being untouched after all this time. I didn't care how sore I was going to be in the morning, I was about to enjoy every minute of this. Gently reaching for my throat, DeAndre pulled me down to him and I kissed him slowly.

Wrapping my arms around his neck, our tongues glided across one another's in a dance that only we knew. His hands were on my ass as he rocked the lower half of my body, grinding me on his dick.

"I missed you so much, baby," I whispered into his mouth. Our intimacy was so intense it made me feel like I was about to burst into tears. Caressing my right cheek, DeAndre looked deeply into my eyes and I saw the man I fell in love with once more. The man that never spoke harshly to me. This was my DeAndre, he was back.

"I love you, always have, always will," he told me, making the tears I tried to hold back roll down my face. Wiping away the tears, DeAndre whispered to me how much he missed the feel of me. We kissed again and the both of us orgasmed together, panting and moaning. Our bodies rejoiced, happy to be reunited again.

Fifteen minutes later we were lying together. I was tucked neatly against DeAndre's side with my head on his chest. This was when I was supposed to mention the building I wanted to lease. This was where I had to tell him that I wanted to start my very own business so I could have a career again.

"Hey, I wanna show you something," he said, tapping me lightly on my shoulder.

"What's that?" I asked, looking up at him.

"Look at this," he told me, averting his eyes down to his feet. I looked down at where he was watching and almost shit in the bed when his toes moved.

"What!?" I shouted excitedly, hopping up in a seated position to get a better look. Cheesing like crazy, I looked on in awe when all of his ten toes moved back and forth.

"Oh my goodness, did this happen today in therapy?" I asked, giddy with excitement.

"Actually, it happened this morning when I was in bed. When Keisha got here I showed it to her. She massaged my legs and we did some stretches. By the time she was done I could move my toes even more. I'm even feeling some tingling in my calves," he gave me an update with a genuine smile I hadn't seen in a while.

I felt as though I was betrayed somehow because he shared his news with Keisha first before me. I knew it was because of how I left him suddenly this morning, so I shouldn't feel any type of way about finding out only now.

"I'm so happy for you, baby." I leaned over to him so I could peck him on his lips before laying down again with my head on his chest.

This moment was too precious for me to change it with news that I knew would shift the mood. At this moment we were happy, and I was prepared not to change it by bringing up something that I knew would cause fireworks. I decided to let it slide tonight.

Unfortunately, things got so much better between us, that one night turned into two nights, then three. I kept procrastinating telling him I wanted to restart my career, loving that my husband was back.

However, the saying all good things must come to an end was about to hit me like a ton of bricks.

CHAPTER TWELVE
CHAOS

The old Chaos was slowly coming back. My legs were actually starting to move again. My wife and I were on the best of terms and the deal breaker...I had a new shipment of cocaine expected in the country in the next few weeks.

It had been almost a month since I regained movement in my toes and a little over a week since I had completely regained feeling in my calves and upper thighs. I even resumed taking therapy at the medical institution. I quit going because I didn't think the sessions were doing shit for me. Keisha would come only once a week to give extra sessions that required strengthening my legs.

Whatever I thought I felt for Keisha disappeared despite the hard-on I got that one time when she massaged me. That incident was a one-time thing and we actually never spoke about it again. I quickly realized that the attraction I felt for her was superficial, but I wasn't sure there was still something about her I couldn't shake.

I looked at the time on my cell because I was waiting for

my wife who was upstairs. I rubbed the well-groomed hair on my chin as I sat on the sofa in the living room. I had been keeping up with regular visits from my barber, looking fresh as fuck. This was the way I knew how to be, looking and feeling like a million dollars.

My hair had grown out quite a bit so instead of rocking the usual low fade, I decided to leave it high at the top with the sides tapered down with a deep line marked to the right. My facial hair was neatly cut, framing my face.

My eyes went to the staircase, wondering again where Beautyful was. We had lunch earlier together and she went upstairs about fifteen minutes ago, telling me she would be right back. I eyed the stairlift, still refusing to use it.

I promised myself I would only go on that thing when my legs could get me in and out of the chair easily and I could walk to our bedroom without the use of my wheelchair. Even though I could get in and out of my chair on my own way better than before, I still wasn't strong enough to walk long distances without my legs weakening and needing to sit down.

I was determined to have myself walking again by next week. I could give a fuck what a nigga had to do... Next week I was getting in my ride and driving to check on my block boys. I needed to let them know that shit was about to be popping for them again. Money would be in their pockets in abundance again pretty soon.

Taking a rolled up blunt from behind my ear, I tapped my pockets in search of my lighter just as I heard footsteps coming down the stairs. With the blunt hanging loosely from my lips, I frowned a little when I saw my wife walking toward me.

She was casually dressed, looking like she was about to head out somewhere. The sound of my lighter sparking up was the only noise in the room as she looked at me. I inhaled deeply as I waited for her to tell me where she was off to.

"You gonna be ok for a few minutes? I need to run off somewhere but I won't be long." She had a sneaky look on her face, and I squinted at her. She giggled at my expression. Taking the blunt from my fingers, she placed it to her pretty ass lips and inhaled.

"Somewhere can be anywhere. I'mma need you to be more specific," I told her, retrieving my blunt from her manicured fingers. One thing I never did was play about my wife. Even in this mothafucking chair in a paralyzed state I would go to war for this woman. Plus, she knew not to play with a nigga.

"I have a surprise for you. When I get back, I'll show you." She cheesed hard at me before bending so she could place a few quick pecks on my mouth.

"The only surprise I need is to know you stopped bleeding so I could get me some of this good-good," I teased her, reaching between her legs, patting her pussy hoping that her period was over.

"Dang, you're so impatient. Five days is not that long," she laughed, swatting my hand away.

"It is for me," I told her, biting into my lower lip. It was funny that before, the thought of having sex was something I wouldn't entertain because of how I felt about my position. Now, I loved the way Beautyful would get on top and ride the fuck out of me. Shit was sexy as fuck.

"Nasty self, yes, it's clear. So get ready for me to leave your ass exhausted later on tonight. I'll be right back," she said, walking toward the front door. I eyed her happily, loving that we were now in a better place than we were a month ago. I really was tripping on Beautyful when all she was trying to do was hold a nigga down.

Seeing that I was on my own for a few, I decided to call my connect to find out how my shipment was coming along. I never mentioned to my wife that I was getting back in the game. I knew we were doing good and this news might knock us back a couple spots.

Beautyful did not want me to go back hitting the streets. She wanted me to sit tight and maybe let Bjorn run shit while I sat behind the scenes. Even though I knew it was wrong, I did agree to her request because I knew it would keep the peace. However, it was nothing short of a mothafucking lie.

I had absolutely no plans of stopping. A bullet in my back wasn't enough to stop a nigga from getting back in the streets and reclaim my spot as being the top cocaine supplier in Philly.

Once Beautyful found out that I was about to pick up right where I left off, shit was about to hit the fan for real. I couldn't help who I was, I was made for the streets. It's in my DNA.

As I was about to make my call, the phone rang and I saw it was my nigga Bjorn.

"My nigga," I answered, pulling on my blunt.

"Sup, I got something to tell you. I know you'll wanna hear this," he spoke up, getting straight to the point.

"What's that?"

"Someone told me that they seen that nigga Pharaoh."

The blunt almost dropped out of my hand and landed on my lap when he said that shit.

"Say word, nigga," I said, sitting up properly on the sofa because I had been waiting for the longest while on this call.

"Word, my nigga. I just got a call from one of our block boys. He said he seen Pharaoh a couple days ago, getting in a heavily tinted BMW truck about two blocks from where I live." Bjorn gave me all the details and my mind was already in overdrive thinking of a way to smoke that fool.

I began rubbing my chin, wondering how I could get my hands on that nigga. On everything, I was about to shoot him twice in his spinal cord and hoped he survived, only to leave him crippled for life.

"You want me to find out more of what the streets are saying? Once I do, I can handle that real quick. Murk that fool and make sure his body is never found."

I was already shaking my head at what Bjorn was offering.

"Na, you know I don't want it to go down like that. I want him myself." I tapped my chest and my voice got dangerously low because murder was on my mind.

"Tell me how you want this to happen then. You know I'm down for whatever."

Dipping my head back, my mouth formed an O, blowing smoke into the air. I had to be sure that my legs were strong enough and soon, I had a nigga to kill.

Tapping my index finger on my lips, I eyed my wife suspiciously as she moved hastily around the kitchen preparing our dinner. Something was definitely up with her and I couldn't wait to hear what her surprise was.

She wore a short baby pink dress that hugged her sexy body. Her hair surrounded her makeup-free face and she smelled like cotton candy. She smiled at me when she caught me admiring her as she plated out my meal.

She placed a couple of pork ribs on my plate along with creamy mashed potatoes and a steamed vegetables medley. I waited for her to be seated in front of her own meal before I started eating. The ambience she set was kind of romantic as there were a couple candles on the table in our spacious kitchen.

Taking a seat opposite me, she blushed before picking up her glass of wine, taking a small sip.

"Well, go ahead and eat up," she encouraged me, picking

up her knife and fork. She began cutting into her meat before taking a bite.

Looking down at my plate, I couldn't even believe she made this dinner from scratch. Before I got shot, cooking was something Beautyful hated to do. I could not begin to say the many times we had an argument over the fact that a nigga never got a meal at least once a week from her.

Now to see just how much she actually enjoyed making meals, especially creating those wild pizza recipes she clearly loved doing so much, was trippy as fuck.

I was really happy that she loved being in the kitchen, seeing that a nigga loved to eat.

"This is really good, babe," I complimented her with my mouth full of food.

"Thank you." She smiled at me mischievously.

"You gonna tell me what's up, or are you gonna let me wait some more?" I asked her, sipping on my wine.

"Ok," she said excitedly, dropping her utensils on her plate. "I got two surprises for you, hold on." Beautiful sprung up from her seat, raced over to the living room, and came back with two envelopes.

Setting them both on the table in front of me, I looked at them curiously as she sat down again, looking on with that stupid grin on her face.

"Open that one first," she said, pointing at the envelope on the right.

"Ok," I replied, doing as she obliged. I picked up the envelope she suggested. Once I got it open I saw it was a brochure for a travel itinerary for a resort in Hawaii.

I smiled and looked up at her because she knew how much I always wanted to go there.

"We're going to Hawaii?" I asked her with an equally stupid grin on my face to match hers.

"We're going to Hawaii!" she exclaimed excitedly, throwing her hands in the air as she laughed.

"That's what's up, ma. When do we leave?" I asked her, and then she made a face that got me worried.

"Well, that's the thing. The travel agency had this particular deal on special. I had to book it so that we can go in the next two and a half weeks. I have faith that you'll be good by then, baby. You'll be walking a lot stronger so we can go strolling on the beach and shit, because we deserve and need this time away."

I wasn't even tripping when she said that because I planned on walking before that anyway.

"You sure right. Hell I'll be running when that time comes. Don't even worry about it," I reassured her with a wink. She squealed with excitement, lunging over the table to kiss me.

"What's this one?" I asked her, rubbing my palms together anticipating the surprise that this envelope had inside.

"Umm, go ahead," she replied in a somewhat hesitant manner.

Reaching for the envelope, I took out what looked to be some sort of contract of sorts. Deep creases formed on my forehead, unsure as to what I was holding.

I began reading, and the more I read the more confused I got.

"I don't understand. Why the fuck did you lease a building for a year?" I asked her, holding the paper in my hand as I looked across at her perplexed.

"Well, I leased it."

"I can see you fucking leased it Beautyful, your name is on the mothafucka. I'm asking why the fuck did you lease it," I was already annoyed because she had this irritating way of answering a question without really answering it.

"Umm," she began, looking down at her hand as she

twisted it nervously on the tabletop. "I mean, you see the way I've been in the kitchen lately, and I'm sure you see how happy it makes me. Not to mention I'm kind of good at it. Sooo...I decided to lease a spot so I can open my own pizza joint."

With my index finger I rubbed the top of my upper lip, looking at the paper in my hand before I focused my attention back on my wife.

"So, you decided to do this without consulting me. While I was in that chair not knowing if I'd ever walk again, you went behind my back and did some sneaky shit like this," I pointed at the paper in my hand, trying my best not to lose my temper because we were having a good night. Plus, we've been getting along really well over the past few weeks, so I wasn't trying to spoil it.

"Sneaky, what's sneaky about me wanting my own career, Chaos?" she asked defensively.

"For starters, according to this document, you signed this shit more than two weeks ago. Why you only now telling me about it?" I asked, putting the document down.

"Why? Because look at you, this is why I kept it from you. Because I knew you were going to overreact, and I was correct!" she began raising her voice as though a nigga was going to get scared.

"Overreact? The only one overreacting here is you. You don't hear me raising my voice, do you?" I told her, taking up my fork so that I could finish my meal.

After a few seconds of me carrying on like she didn't just share something important with me, she interrupted my chewing.

"Well, aren't we going to discuss this further?" she questioned me, which confused me.

"We just discussed it."

"What? When did we have a discussion?" she asked with an annoyed expression.

"Just now. The answer is no. Get out of the lease. I can't wait for our Hawaii trip though, that shit about to be lit," I told her with my mouth full of food. Judging from the look on her face, she did not appreciate my answer.

"*No*, why no? Oh wait, let me guess, because Chaos said so, right?"

I placed my fork down, still managing to keep my anger in check even though she was really trying me.

"Why do you find the need to work, Beautyful? I provide you with everything any female would love to have. You don't want for a mothafucking thing. Before we got married, I told you the kind of wife I wanted and you agreed. Now, here we are three years later and you drop some silly shit like this on me. The answer isn't just no...it's fuck no!" I started to lose my patience and my voice went up a couple of levels.

"Chaos, you know I never really wanted this kept lifestyle. I've always worked, you met me working. I just want to feel as though I'm not walking in your shadow anymore. I want my own identity." She tapped her chest, and I narrowed my eyes at her menacingly.

"Where the fuck is all this coming from? You got somebody in your ear? Who is it? Lovely or Toni, or maybe is both them bitches!" I barked at her.

"Don't!" She pounded the palm of her hand on the tabletop with a loud bang. "Do not disrespect my family and my friend." She gritted her teeth, pointing her index finger at me.

"Nobody is not in my ear. I don't need to have a cheer squad in my corner to know what I want. I've always been on your side, supporting you and being there for you. I ask for this one thing and you can't let me have it. What do I have, Chaos? There's only so much shopping and spa days a bitch can stomach. I've even expressed that we should think about starting a family. You've turned down that idea too. Saying it's not the right time because we all know whatever Chaos wants, Chaos gets!"

Beautyful was really beginning to piss a nigga off.

"This conversation is beginning to bore me and I don't particularly appreciate you shouting at me. Let's finish our meal and go to bed, so we can kiss and make up," I told her, picking the signed lease up and placing it back inside of the envelope.

Beautyful began laughing like some sort of maniac with a crazed look in her eyes.

"I am not giving up that building just because you want me to." I could see her nostrils flare in and out, which only amused me further.

"You wanna bet?"

"Fuck you, Chaos," she sneered at me.

"That's what I've been trying to do. You ready for us to take this fight to the bedroom?" I licked my lips in a lustful manner, which I knew would only piss her off further.

"You think this is funny?" she asked, narrowing her eyes at me.

"Hilarious actually." I rubbed my chin, refusing to get worked up by this.

"Do you know why this marriage works for you? Because you make all the rules. I've never had a say in anything, and I should have put a stop to that from the start, so I blame myself. I've been there for you in more ways than one, but this is where I put my foot down. You are not taking this from me. Think I haven't heard you talking to Bjorn, planning to get back out in the streets after I nearly lost you? After you told me you wouldn't go back out there. When will it be enough, Chaos? This insatiable thirst for power." I could hear the sadness in her voice, but that wasn't about to change my mind.

"You knew who you were marrying, the streets are my life. As I said, we agreed on what I wanted my wife to be and you're not about to go back on that just because you've been in the kitchen for a couple days. Get the fuck outta here with that shit," I dismissed her with a wave of my hand.

The first teardrop trickled down her right cheek and she pushed her chair back loudly, getting to her feet. Marching over to my side of the table, she snatched the envelope that held her lease. Bending her body so we were now eye level, she opened her mouth to speak.

"You can go fuck yourself tonight," she whispered before she stood up to make her dramatic exit.

I listened to her livid footsteps making their way through the living room and then she angrily stomped up the stairs.

I guess I'm about to sleep alone tonight, I thought to myself with a shake of my head, confused as to how our dinner got fucked so fast. Resting the palms of my hands flat on the table, I took my time as I slowly got out of my seat.

With shaky, cautious baby steps, I walked to my wheelchair that was a couple feet away and eased myself in.

It was safe to say dinner was now over. I needed to take my ass to bed...alone.

My arm rested on my forehead as I lay on my back staring at the ceiling in the bedroom. Sleep refused to come find me, I'm guessing because my wife wasn't by my side. As suspected, she never came to bed tonight because of the fight we had.

Now, here was my goofy ass wide awake at 3 a.m. Not to

mention I was horny as hell and my dick was now standing at attention in my boxers.

"Jesus," I mumbled in frustration as I squeezed the crotch of my boxers. My eyes roamed the room, thinking I should buss one off so I wouldn't wake up with blue balls in the morning.

Needing some inspiration, my eyes caught sight of the Ring cam strategically placed on a small bookshelf in the corner of the room. When you were a man of my profession security was a big fucking deal. I had cameras in just about every room in my home.

Since Beautyful began sleeping with me regularly, I decided to turn the camera turned off, just because. However, there was the one time she came in here unexpectedly wearing her naughty lingerie along with her sex toy. That would have been recorded that night.

Reaching for my phone, I found the Ring app and searched, looking for that particular day. I smiled broadly when I found the recording date for the day I wanted. As I looked at the screen, something caught my eyes and I had to do a double take.

Pausing the video, I squinted in the darkness of the room, not sure if I was seeing correctly.

"What the fuck was she doing in my room?" I asked nobody as I stared at the screen with Keisha on it. Hitting play, I allowed the video to continue the recording as Keisha was oblivious to the fact that she was being taped.

I tried jogging my memory back to this day, and then it hit me. This was the day of our second session when she massaged me and my dick betrayed me by getting hard. I remember her excusing herself, telling me she needed to use the bathroom.

She had been gone close to ten minutes before she returned to the gym. She jokingly said she wanted to give me enough time to get it together before she returned. Now I see why she took so fucking long; it was because she was snooping in my room. The question was...why?

As the video played, I watched as Keisha searched relentlessly, making sure she put everything back exactly how she got it. Taking her phone out, she made a call and began talking to someone.

"I don't see anything...yes, I looked everywhere... Maybe it's in the bedroom upstairs, but I've been gone way too long, he'll suspect something. I gotta go," I listened to her conversation as I tried to figure out who the fuck was this bitch.

As I looked on and she began to make her exit from out of my bedroom, reality slapped my dumb ass in my face.

"Mothafucka," I whispered, pausing the video and zooming in on her face. I finally knew why I couldn't shake the feeling I got the moment I saw this bitch. It was because I saw her face before. All this time I believed it was some attraction I had for her but no, it wasn't that.

I saw her face saved as a caller ID for the person I'd been searching for, for the past four months. The person that set me up and was the reason why I ended up in a wheelchair. I jogged my memory back to a day when Pharaoh and I were in the middle of a transaction.

His phone rang and when he took it out, I recalled seeing the word wifey on the screen with a picture of his bitch. The female was Keisha. I remembered thinking that his girl was fine but not as fine as mine.

Dumb shit like that was the reason I always told Beautyful not to call me when I was handling my drops. Getting caught was as simple as one phone call.

The bigger question was did she know who I was all this time? The next thing I needed to know was what the fuck she was looking for.

Putting my phone away, I linked my fingers behind my head and laid back on my pillow with a wide smile on my face. Keisha was due to visit tomorrow at exactly noon. My smile grew even wider. Tomorrow was about to be one good mothafucking day.

CHAPTER THIRTEEN
BEAUTYFUL

I sniffed loudly, using the back of my hand to wipe under my nose as I lay in bed. A tub of Haagen Daz ice cream resting on my stomach as I watched the movie *The Best Man Holiday*.

I was at the part of the movie when they found out Mia was dying, and I was crying my eyes out as though I hadn't watched this show like a hundred fucking times.

Why couldn't I have the kind of marriage that Mia and Lance shared? I asked myself, dipping my spoon into the dulce de leche ice cream. I felt, my eyes grow misty as Lance scored his touchdown and now he had to race home to be by his wife's side.

I remembered when Chaos proposed to me. We had only been together about nine months. We were at his parents' home celebrating their anniversary. The next thing I knew, as everyone was eating their dessert, which was peach cobbler, I almost choked to death when my greedy ass almost ate the engagement ring he had his mother place in my slice.

He got down on one knee, laughing after he helped me pry

the ring from my mouth. I cried tears of happiness when I told him yes, I would be his wife, as he slipped the ring on my finger with the huge diamond. His family cheered and congratulated us.

The next couple of months of planning our wedding, I remembered not having much of a say to anything. Chaos hired a wedding planner, telling me he didn't want me getting stressed out with organizing the wedding, fearing I would turn into *bridezilla*.

I recall telling him I didn't mind, but he insisted that I left it to the experts. Maybe I should have been more persistent. Maybe this was where our problems started, where I began to lose my voice and allowed him to silence me when I preferred to be heard.

Our wedding was like a page out of a fairytale. It was extravagant and cost well over 150K. My dress was from one of the top designers, a name that I couldn't even pronounce. We wrote our vows and I cried when I read mine to him.

Our wedding song had us giggling throughout our dance, which confused our guests. We whispered to each other as we recalled the first time we danced to Aaliyah's song Let Me Know and the orgasm that he gave me. Our wedding was a night I would never forget, even if I lived to be one hundred years old and was afflicted with Alzheimer's. I would still remember our special day.

Chaos didn't lie when he said he told me the kind of wife he wanted or rather, preferred me to be. He made it abundantly clear his wife would never need to work. Not only because he did not want her to, but because she wouldn't have to.

At first that shit was dope as fuck to me. What woman wouldn't want a man to give her the world and then some? Credit cards with an unlimited balance, expensive dinner dates, picking out any car my heart desired at dealerships, lavish vacations. The whole nine yards, I loved every minute of it.

However, what was a woman to do when her husband wanted to rule the world? The millions he made weren't enough. He wanted and craved for more. I wanted dumb things like his time and to start a family, while he wanted more money, an endless supply of cocaine, and for his name to be infamous in the streets.

Chaos never cared about how I felt and what I wanted. Control and power were his drug. As much as I loved my husband, deciding to no longer allow him to dictate my every move was something I needed to do.

"Oh, don't cry, Lance," I spoke to the TV as Morris collapsed on top of Mia's grave.

My phone suddenly began ringing on the bed next to me. Seeing it was my sister, I decided to ignore her call because I was in no mood to speak to anyone.

However, she called again back to back, and something told me that I should see what she wanted. Sighing heavily, I swiped the screen.

"Lovely," I tried not to let my voice reflect what I was going through and feeling.

"Have you spoken to Toni today?" she asked me with somewhat of a panicked voice.

"No, why, is something wrong?" I asked her, sticking the spoon inside the tub of ice cream.

"Did her son's daycare call you? They called me saying they couldn't reach you after Toni didn't show to pick Aiden up from daycare." Lovely had my full attention now and I sat upright in my bed.

"Shit, maybe they called when I was in the bathroom a

short while ago. What's going on?" I was already throwing the covers off my body so I could get out of bed.

"I'm not sure, but I'm on my way to get him. You know Toni do not play about that child. So the fact that she did not show up to pick him up says that something isn't right. When was the last time you spoke to her?" Lovely's question had me cursing myself.

Lovely and I made it our business to never let a week go by without speaking to our friend. Keeping in touch with Toni constantly could literally mean life or death. I was so wrapped up in all I had been dealing with, with my husband. It hadn't dawned on me that it had been more than a week since I last spoke with my friend.

"Shit, it's been a minute. Do you think she's relapsed? Did you reach out to work?" I asked, deciding I needed to get dressed so I could meet up with my sister and go check on Toni.

"I dunno, maybe. Leaving Aiden stranded is something she's never done. Yeah, I called her job and spoke to her secretary, she said she called in sick two days straight," Lovely was right. Toni would never leave her son stranded at school, so something had to be wrong.

"You're right. I'll meet you at Toni's." We said our goodbyes before hanging up.

I stumbled across the bedroom to get dressed because I'd been laying around moping in my underwear all day. Grabbing up the first pieces of clothing I found, I shoved my legs into a pair of denim shorts and a white Lacoste t-shirt. Slipping a pair of Prada sneakers on my feet, I ran over to look at myself in the mirror. I nearly screamed in fright at the bird's nest on my head for hair. Grabbing a brush, I proceeded to put my hair into a bun, leaving my bangs out.

Finding the keys to my Lincoln Navigator, I picked up my

phone and began my descent down the stairs. I tried calling Toni then, but her phone just rang out.

"Oh, Toni," I mumbled worriedly, praying that she hadn't spiraled down back into that dark rabbit hole. I hadn't been downstairs for the day, except to get the ice cream, so Chaos and I hadn't spoken since last night. There was no sign of him as I walked through the living room, heading toward the front door.

I thanked God for that, because the last thing I was in the mood for was him asking me questions I didn't wish to answer. Believing that I was home free, I placed my hand on the doorknob and began to twist it open.

"Going somewhere?" his raspy voice asked from behind me.

You couldn't let me have this one, O Lord, I said to myself as I looked up at the Heavens. Exhaling loudly because I was in no mood for him and his bullshit, I slowly turned around to face him.

He sat in his chair about to light a blunt as he waited for my answer.

"Lovely just called me. We think something's wrong with Toni. She didn't pick her son up today, the school called. We're gonna make sure she's alright." I decided to be as clear as I could because he knew Toni's situation. I shared it with him after we got married.

"Ok cool, go handle that," he replied with a nod of his head. Just as I turned the knob once more, his voice spoke up again. "Did you speak with the realtor today to see if you can get out of the lease?"

"I'll see you when I get back," was my response. Not bothering to turn around, I walked out the door.

Hopping into my Lincoln, I drove out of our six-car garage to make my way to Toni's. I literally had to force myself not to think about Chaos as I drove. Never have I felt this hopeless and lost in my life.

"Shit," I mumbled, realizing that I needed gas. Looking over at the passenger seat where I usually kept my handbag or purse, I made a face when I saw the spot was empty.

"Double shit," I mumbled again, sucking my teeth, annoyed with myself that I now had to turn back. Sighing softly, I looked at the time and calculated it should take me about fifteen minutes to make it back to the house. Signaling, I made a risky move in order to turn my car around. I got a few angry words from other drivers, but it didn't matter to me.

As I got closer to the house, I saw a car parked in our driveway. At first I thought Bjorn had dropped by for a visit but as I got closer, I realized it was Keisha's ride.

I had been so preoccupied with finding out what happened to Toni that it totally slipped my mind that Chaos had a session with Keisha today. He had been improving really well since he resumed therapy at the medical office. Therefore, Keisha's sessions had been cut to just once a week.

I decided that I would just run quickly up to my room with hopes of not being seen by either of them. So that's exactly what I did. Racing up the stairs, I found my Gucci purse on the nightstand. Doing a quick check to make sure I had enough cash and my credit cards were inside, I began making my way back down the stairs.

I'm not sure what it was, but my steps to the front door began to slow for no apparent reason. Until I came to a complete stop and I turned in the direction that would take me to the gym.

It was like an invisible magnetic force was pulling me down the corridor toward the gym door. I stepped lightly, barely making a sound until I was standing in front of the wooden barrier with my hand on the doorknob.

My heart pounded loudly, echoing in my ear, then it plummeted to the floor when I opened the door and looked inside. The back of my neck burned with anger, rage, and possibly shame at the sight of Keisha on her knees. DeAndre was seated in his wheelchair and from where I stood, his dick appeared to be down the back of Keisha's throat.

He had a weird look on his face as he watched Keisha between his legs committing adultery. Everything that happened after was all a big blur. I have no recollection of moving my feet. All I knew I had Keisha pinned to the ground on her back as I decked her repeatedly in her face.

Cursing at her, being sure to let her know she was a fucking hoe. Her screams bounced off the walls in the gym as I slammed her head into the floor. I was on the verge of committing my first murder.

"Stop, stop. It's not what you think, Beautyful," I heard Chaos say before I felt his hands prying me off Keisha.

"Get the fuck off me!" I yelled at him, shoving him away and hopping to my feet. I looked down at both DeAndre and Keisha. Chaos rubbed his back as he grimaced in pain while Keisha was a bloody and swollen mess.

My chest heaved up and down in anger as I focused on this trifling heffa.

"Bitch, get the fuck out my house before I go upstairs, get my 9mm, and kill your mothafucking ass," I spat at her, wanting to jump on her again to finish what I started.

"I'm so sorry," Keisha apologized, holding her leaking nose. Scrambling to her feet, she zoomed past me fast as fuck and raced out the door.

Now it was just me and my cheating ass husband. I looked down at him in disgust. I didn't see when he managed to put his dick back inside of his pants, but it was no longer out. He kept rubbing his back with a pained expression as he sat on the floor in an uncomfortable position.

"How long have you been fucking your therapist?" I asked, tempted to kick him straight in his face.

"The fuck are you talking about? I'm not fucking Keisha. Jesus, can you help me up from off the floor so I can explain?" He kept rubbing his back and he began to look as though he might pass out. His complexion grew pale as he grunted with discomfort. He then stared up at me like he was actually waiting for me to help his sorry ass up from the floor.

Hot tears ran down my cheeks as I felt sick to my stomach. I couldn't be in the same house with this man, far less the same room.

"I'll go upstairs and pack some stuff. I'll be staying with either Lovely or my dad until I can get a place of my own," I told him, wiping my cheeks as I sniffed back the water that almost trickled out my nose.

The look on his face when I told him I was leaving him was one I'll never forget. DeAndre struggled to stand on his wobbly feet and I didn't wait to see if he would be successful or not. Bolting out of the room, I half jogged, half walked down the corridor toward the stairs.

"Beautyful!" DeAndre shouted my name, which I purposely ignored.

I took the stairs two at a time even as more tears blinded my vision. With clumsy, shaky legs, I made it to our bedroom and found a huge overnight bag. I began shoving clothes, shoes, and toiletries inside, not really paying too much attention to what was being placed in my getaway bag.

My body was numb and so was my brain. I wasn't even sure I'd fully comprehended what was happening. I was so caught up in my thoughts that I hadn't realized I was no longer alone.

"Aye."

Dumbfounded, I turned to the voice and there he was. Standing, he leaned up on the doorframe looking as though simply being on his feet was the hardest thing he had ever done. DeAndre had finally made it up the stairs after all these months. After the many attempts I made to get him up here... he made it. And all it took was for me to catch his good for nothing ass getting his dick sucked.

We stood just looking at each other before his eyes went to the bag on the bed. He immediately snapped out of his trance.

"I-I used the stairlift. It wasn't so bad after all," he said, taking a couple wobbly steps inside of the bedroom. His legs still weren't very strong. I was certain that just standing there was very strenuous on his lower back and would tire him out soon.

"Good for you," I replied, not giving a fuck, if he did back flips to get up those stairs or not. Zipping the bag closed and grabbing the straps, I was ready to leave, never to step foot in this house again.

"You need to let me explain." DeAndre's voice had dropped a couple notches as he slowly made his way to our bed. The bed he refused to climb into with me for the last few months. Groaning, he sat down with an exaggerated sigh, looking at me with pleading eyes.

"Explain why I saw Keisha on her knees sucking your dick? What... what explanation is needed about that? Oh no, wait, you're about to tell me that she slipped and your dick accidentally ended up down her throat. After all I did for you. After all I endured these months. You turn around and do me like this. You gave up all we had away for a random bitch, willing to drop to her knees and suck your dick." I wanted to scream at him, punch him in the face, scratch his eyes out. Instead, I was going to leave with dignity even if my heart was breaking into a million pieces inside.

"Loving someone is wonderful, but when you love that person more than you love yourself is when it all goes downhill. That was me, Chaos. I loved you more than I loved myself. You got everything you wanted time after time. You got the trophy wife that you could show off and take care of just as long as she does what you say.

"You get control and power in the streets. You wanted to be the biggest drug dealer Philly has ever seen...and you got that. Meanwhile, what did I get, Chaos? You think I don't know how this is about to go once you get strong enough and you're out of that wheelchair? It's back to my husband loving the streets and spending time on the corners more than he does with his wife. Once again, me wanting stupid shit like starting a family and having my man home is going to get pushed on the back burner." I poured my heart out as I twisted and turned the wedding ring on my finger.

Huffing loudly, DeAndre pinched between his eyes as he shook his head.

"I just need a few minutes for this fucking pain to subside and I'll explain myself." I rolled my eyes because if he used the word explain one more time, I'd get the gun out the dresser and shoot him in his back again.

"When you put this ring on my finger, I swear that was the happiest day of my life." Slipping the wedding ring off, my heart shattered all over again as I looked at it in the palm of my hand. Walking to the dresser, I placed the ring on top of it and picked up a bottle of DeAndre's pain medication.

Grabbing up my bag, I handed him the bottle so he could take his meds.

"There you go, you look as though you really need those," I

told him, handing him the bottle that he slowly took from my outstretched hand.

"Think I'm gonna let you leave me, Beautyful?" he said, his voice barely audible as he fidgeted to open the bottle.

"The way I see it, you don't have much of a choice unless you plan to get up from off that bed and run behind me," I said sarcastically, and he eyed me angrily as he threw a couple pills down the back of his throat.

"Goodbye, Chaos."

I heard him struggle to call out to me as I walked out of the room. I even heard him attempting to get up from the bed. Even if he was successful in making it down the stairs, I would be long gone by then.

Never looking back, I made my way out the front door and into my ride. I had no idea when I drove out of the driveway until the tears were too much, blinding my vision making it hard for me to see the road. Cursing myself and not to mention the day I met Chaos; I pulled over to the side of the street.

Covering my face with my hands, I shook uncontrollably, never feeling any pain like this before as I cried alone in my car. How did this happen? How did my life went to shit in such a short space of time was fucking crazy to me. What if I never forgot my purse and had to return to the house? Chaos may have found a way to fuck the shit out of Keisha with his handicapped ass.

The ringing of my phone on the passenger seat brought me out of my meltdown. Wiping my eyes and nose, I reached for it and made a face. It was Sabrina. Believing she was calling about Keisha, the hoe she sent to work at my home, I answered her call ready to cuss her ass out.

"Hello," I said, putting the phone on speaker, resting my forehead on the steering wheel. My car was still running.

"What's up, Beautyful? Is your sister with you like right

now by chance?" Sabrina's question made me scrunch my face up.

"Why are you asking about Lovely? Didn't you call about Keisha?" I asked, confused.

"No, why will I be calling about Keisha? Did she do something?" Sabrina asked. For a quick second, my mouth opened to spill all the tea, but then I quickly changed my mind. I didn't need a stranger to know that my marriage was falling apart.

"No she didn't do anything. And Lovely is not with me, I am on my way to meet her though. What's this call about?" I asked, wanting to end this conversation so I could continue crying in peace.

Sabrina hesitated for a few seconds before she began talking. "Um, I don't usually get into people's business or whatever, but you're cool people. I'm about to send you a video of a party I was at last night. These kinds of parties are usually attended by an elite crowd. No video footage is allowed, pictures, none of that." Sabrina was going on and on and I still had no idea what her phone call was about.

"I don't mean to be rude, but what does any of this have to do with my sister?" I asked, getting ready to hang the phone up on her.

"You'll see when I send the video. I'll talk to you later."

Before I could say anything she ended the call, and right after a message with a video attached popped up on my screen.

Still not sure why she sent this to me, I hit play on the video. Turning my phone, I watched the footage she sent and got even more confused when Dorian, Lovely's husband, appeared on my screen. He sat on a sofa in what looked to be a club of some sort. He had no clue he was being filmed as he sipped on something in a plastic cup.

There were a lot of other people around, both men and women. Suddenly, a man came, taking a seat next to Dorian.

They began talking but of course I couldn't hear what was being said.

My jaw hit my chest when Dorian unzipped his pants and the white man with long, curly auburn hair dropped his head and began sucking his dick right there like nobody's business in the crowded club. The party was some sort of gay swinger's type shit. In the background men were kissing men and women were kissing women.

Dipping his head back, Dorian closed his eyes as he put his hand behind the man's head, shoving his face further down into his lap. Then the video stopped.

My mouth remained open as I stared at my phone in utter shock.

"Dorian's gay," I muttered to myself. As if this day couldn't get any fucking worse!

To be continued....

ALSO BY CANDY MOORE

The Wife Of A Jamaican Billionaire 3
The Wife Of A Jamaican Billionaire 2
The Wife Of A Jamaican Billionaire

Made in United States
Orlando, FL
29 April 2024